"How can you ... asked

Carson swallowed hard and studied his boots. He didn't have a clue how to answer. Madeline's rigid shoulders and defiant eyes suggested she was as uncomfortable with this conversation as he was.

"You saved my life," Madeline whispered. "You took me into your home. Why not lock me up in protective custody? Why are you helping me? Save yourself the grief."

"I thought I hated you. I thought I should hate you. You aren't your father. You're not responsible for what he did." He almost said how much he liked looking at her, how much he wanted to hold her and kiss her.

Madeline ducked her head and lowered her eyelids. Her shy, sideways look sent rational thought from his head. A small voice told him he tread dangerous waters, but he longed to feel the texture of her skin.

He couldn't help himself. When she lifted her face, he kissed her....

Dear Harlequin Intrigue Reader,

We have a superb lineup of outstanding romantic suspense this month starting with another round of QUANTUM MEN from Amanda Stevens. A *Silent Storm* is brewing in Texas and it's about to break....

More great series continue with Harper Allen's MEN OF THE DOUBLE B RANCH trilogy. A *Desperado Lawman* has his hands full with a spitfire who is every bit his match. As well, B.J. Daniels adds the second installment to her CASCADES CONCEALED miniseries with *Day of Reckoning*.

In *Secret Witness* by Jessica Andersen, a woman finds herself caught between a rock—a killer threatening her child—and a hard place—the detective in charge of the case. What will happen when she has to make the most inconceivable choice any woman can make?

Launching this month is a new promotion we are calling COWBOY COPS. Need I say more? Look for *Behind the Shield* by veteran Harlequin Intrigue author Sheryl Lynn. And newcomer, Rosemary Heim, contributes to DEAD BOLT with *Memory Reload*.

Enjoy!

Sincerely,

Denise O'Sullivan
Senior Editor
Harlequin Intrigue

BEHIND THE SHIELD
SHERYL LYNN

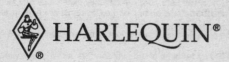

HARLEQUIN®

TORONTO • NEW YORK • LONDON
AMSTERDAM • PARIS • SYDNEY • HAMBURG
STOCKHOLM • ATHENS • TOKYO • MILAN • MADRID
PRAGUE • WARSAW • BUDAPEST • AUCKLAND

ISBN 0-373-22763-9

BEHIND THE SHIELD

Copyright © 2004 by Jaye W. Manus

Visit us at www.eHarlequin.com

Printed in U.S.A.

ABOUT THE AUTHOR

Sheryl Lynn lives in a pine forest atop a hill in Colorado. When not writing, she amuses herself by embarrassing her two teenagers, walking her dogs in a nearby park and feeding peanuts to the dozens of Steller's jays, scrub jays, blue jays and squirrels who live in her backyard. Her best ideas come from the newspapers, although she admits that a lot of what she reads is way too weird for fiction.

Books by Sheryl Lynn

HARLEQUIN INTRIGUE
190—DOUBLE VISION
223—DEADLY DEVOTION
258—SIMON SAYS
306—LADYKILLER
331—DARK KNIGHT*
336—DARK STAR*
367—THE OTHER LAURA
385—BULLETPROOF HEART
424—THE CASE OF THE VANISHED GROOM†
425—THE CASE OF THE BAD LUCK FIANCÉ†
467—EASY LOVING
514—THE BODYGUARD†
518—UNDERCOVER FIANCÉ†
608—TO PROTECT THEIR CHILD**
612—COLORADO'S FINEST**
763—BEHIND THE SHIELD

*Mirror Images
†Honeymoon Hideaway/Elk River, Colorado
**McClintock Country

Don't miss any of our special offers. Write to us at the following address for information on our newest releases.

Harlequin Reader Service
U.S.: 3010 Walden Ave., P.O. Box 1325, Buffalo, NY 14269
Canadian: P.O. Box 609, Fort Erie, Ont. L2A 5X3

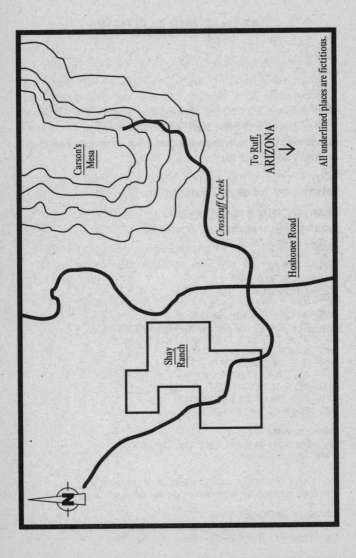

Carson's
Mesa

Crossruff Creek

Shay
Ranch

Hoshonee Road

To Ruff,
ARIZONA
→

All underlined places are fictitious.

CAST OF CHARACTERS

Police Chief Carson Cody—A cowboy cop who can't allow his shattered heart to stand in the way of duty.

Madeline Shay—A half-Apachean artist who can't hide from her family's legacy of destruction.

Frank Shay—He was evil in life and pure trouble in death.

Tony Rule—This gorgeous, wealthy bad boy will do anything to get close to the lovely Madeline.

Ivan Bannerman—An insurance fraud investigator looking to commit a few frauds of his own.

Judy Green—She can't stand seeing Carson lonely and bereft, and would like nothing better than to fill the void in his life.

Maurice Harrigan—The mayor of Ruff yearns for vengeance for the death of his son, and since the father is dead, the daughter makes the perfect target.

This is for Denise O'Sullivan,
who loves cowboy cops as much as I do.
Thank you for the inspiration, m'dear.
Thank you, too, to the kind folks at Chins Up
who have filled my cup to overflowing
and put footsteps on my stairs again.
And of course, as always, thank you, Tom,
for always being my rock.

Chapter One

"Back off, boyo. Today is not the day to bug him." Shaking her head, with an expression of dire warning, the dispatcher held the arm of the young officer.

Wanda spoke softly, but Chief Carson Cody heard. Annoyance prickled his scalp.

It irritated the devil out of him to witness the pity he saw on every face this morning. It started with Judy, the woman who came to his house three days a week to clean, cook and do the laundry. Instead of her usual chatter, Judy had greeted him with a cloud of worry in her eyes.

She acted as if she expected him to go berserk and start shooting up the town.

Folks stared when he drove the cruiser along Ruff's Main Street. Nobody waved or shouted a greeting. In the rearview mirror he caught quite a few heads bent together in whispered conversations. Even old Luke, the aged war veteran who hung around the courthouse, engaging passersby in arguments, looked away when Carson climbed the steps.

As he entered his office, Wanda said, "It's the anniversary of...you know."

Carson took care not to slam the door.

Anniversary. Like some twisted antiholiday. All the town of Ruff needed were banners strung across Main Street. They could offer prizes for the first person who spotted Ruff's police chief cracking up.

He aimed his white Stetson for the hat rack, but paused.

Who was he trying to kid? He hadn't been right for a year. Today drove home how not right he was. For the past few weeks, as this *anniversary* approached, an unnerving, unbalanced sensation grew stronger, stripping the landscape of color, robbing his voice of inflection and his thoughts of coherency. He slept poorly. Food lost its flavor. He sleepwalked through his days, doing his job by rote. He settled the cowboy hat back on his head.

"I'm taking a personal day, Wanda," he said. "Pete can handle anything that comes up."

Behind oversize glasses sparkling with rhinestones, her eyes were grim, searching. "Okay, Chief."

He grew aware of stares. When he glanced around the big room crowded with desks and filing cabinets, everyone suddenly got busy. Keyboards clacked. Files rustled. Chair wheels squeaked. Even the window fans seemed to hum louder.

"I'm okay," he told the dispatcher.

"I know that." Her wide eyes called him a liar.

CARSON STOOD on the bank of Crossruff Creek. He didn't want to be here—he needed to be here. Water riffled over the rocky streambed. By mid-June the creek would be barely a whisper and the grasses, now so fragile green, would be tall and dry yellow. Cottonwood trees lined the creek. Gusts of wind turned the leaves inside out and silver. A hawk soared overhead in lazy circles. Fresh deer tracks wove through stands of scrubby oaks and piñon pines, and crisscrossed stretches of sand.

Too pretty a place for dying. He rubbed his eyes with the pads of his fingers.

Footsteps alerted him. He placed a hand on the butt of the .45 holstered on his hip. Skeeters darted across the water in an insect version of the Ice Capades.

A branch snapped. He couldn't muster enough energy to turn around to see who approached. The hawk's shadow passed the ground in front of him. He watched the bird fold its wings and dive.

"This is a real pretty place," a woman said. "Much too pretty for suicide."

He didn't recognize the voice, which was soft and low and cool as spring water. He turned his head enough to see the speaker. She rested a shoulder against the gnarled trunk of a cottonwood and folded her arms. She wore jeans with blown knees and a white T-shirt. Two black braids, gleaming as if oiled, hung over her shoulders. She was Indian, maybe, or Hispanic, but not Navajo. Her face struck a chord of memory, but he couldn't place it. It bothered him. He never forgot a face.

He touched fingers to the brim of his hat. "Pardon, ma'am, but I'm not suicidal."

"You have the look. Sorry."

Sorry he had the look? Sorry she'd mentioned it? He failed to rouse enough energy to really care what she meant.

Then it hit him who she was. A fist strangled his guts. His throat tightened so he thought he might choke. Such violence of emotion scared him. Maybe the townsfolk were right. Maybe he was about to crack.

"What are you doing here?"

Her eyebrows lifted at his churlish question. "I live here."

He stared unseeing at the water. He wasn't the easiest of men when it came to socializing, but his mother had taught him how to be polite even when provoked. That he wanted to yell at this woman, vent his rage and despair and grief, well, it was unsettling.

"I didn't mean to startle you," she said.

"I heard you coming."

Brave or foolish, or both, she pushed away from the cottonwood and stood next to him. She was tall, and her arms were finely muscled. The ragged jeans fit snugly over graceful hips and long legs. Under normal circumstances he'd give this woman a second look on the street, maybe a third and fourth look. She was striking enough to warrant wayward thoughts.

But she wasn't worth knowing.

"Madeline Shay," he said. Her name was dirt in his mouth.

"Chief Cody," she said in return. She sighed. "Is this where it happened?"

He did not want to talk about it. Not now, and not with her. He couldn't fathom why she was here. If he didn't leave he'd do something stupid. He tipped his hat again.

"I am so very sorry," she said.

The words were meaningless, but the undiluted sorrow behind them drained the anger like pulling a plug.

Oh, God, but he was tired. If he lay down and closed his eyes, he might sleep a year. Or ten years. Sleep through all these agonizing anniversaries until the pain dissipated under its own weight. He sank to the ground, facing the creek, and drew up his knees to rest his arms across them. Madeline sat, too, on the grass, with her back to him and hugging her knees. It didn't seem possible she hurt as much as he, but it might be so.

"I'm sorry, too," he said.

"Do you know why he did it?"

Anger flashed again. "Is that why you've come? Morbid curiosity?"

She turned her head. A fine hand had sculpted her profile into strong features and smooth planes. Her skin was more golden than brown and a fine spray of freckles banded her nose. "No."

"Then why are you here? In this place? On this day?"

If his anger affected her, she hid it. "Actually I've been here a few weeks. And I came down because I saw your car on the road." She pointed east, up the mesa. "You live there? I see the lights at night."

A few weeks. It didn't seem possible. Ruff, Arizona, was a small community in the midst of rugged mountains and mesas. Folks paid attention to the comings and goings of locals and tourists. Gossip was the favored pastime. Madeline Shay's presence should make front-page news.

"I've been keeping a low profile," she said.

Odd, but not illegal. Or not odd, considering what kind of reception she'd receive if she set foot in town. When she collected her father's body last year, she'd been accosted on the steps of the funeral home. Calls came in to the police station warning that Madeline Shay was a dead woman if the sun set while she was still in Ruff.

He plucked a blade of new grass and stuck the sweet, pithy end in his mouth. "Low profile or not, this isn't the healthiest place for you."

Her shoulders rose and fell in a silent sigh. "Healthy or not, it's mine. I tried to sell it, but there isn't a real estate agent within two hundred miles who'll return my calls."

He grunted.

"I promise—I won't be here more than a few months, Chief Cody. I won't cause any trouble. I need a place to work."

That she was Frank Shay's daughter made him sick and angry and wanting to throw back his head and howl in rage. But being who she was broke no laws. He couldn't throw her off her own property. If either was in the wrong, he was for trespassing.

She rose and dusted off the seat of her jeans. "I'll leave you to your thoughts, sir. Sorry to disturb you."

When she faced him, sunshine lit her face. Her eyes were a pale shade of rusty green, striking against her honey-skinned face. Clear, sad eyes that met his straight on. He wondered where her steadiness came from. Not from her father and, from the little he knew, it hadn't come from her mother, either.

She asked, "Was it you?"

The question caught him off guard. He knew what she meant.

"You're the one who shot him."

He cursed his own imagination and how easily he conjured every detail. Frank Shay crashing through the brush, his breath like a freight train chugging up a hill. Waving the pistol and screaming, "It's not me! I didn't do it!" A prickly pear pad clung to his jeans. A funny detail, but Carson remembered.

"I did." He knew what would haunt his dreams tonight.

She looked away. "When I got word he'd been

killed, I wasn't all that surprised. Some people wear a bad end like a hat. You know dying of old age isn't for them.''

Carson wondered if she was assuring him she didn't blame him for her father's death. It didn't matter if she did or didn't. If Frank Shay miraculously reappeared, Carson would be more than happy to kill him again. Only this time it wouldn't be a clean shot. This time Shay would suffer.

''He sent letters from prison. I ignored them. If I'd been a better daughter, if I'd written back, visited, things might have turned out different.''

Frank Shay was the closest thing to pure evil Carson had ever known. ''Doubt it,'' he said.

She turned around and tucked her hands into the back pockets of her jeans. Carson noticed scars along the tender inside of her upper arms. Round, puckered scars with that unmistakable stain of old burns. His gut clenched.

''You're right. He wasn't a good man. He hurt people even when he didn't mean to hurt them. It's just that...he told me things were different. If I'd given him another chance none of this would have happened. I am so sorry.''

He wanted very much to hate her, to freely grant her the blame. With Frank Shay dead and buried, Carson had no target for the rage eating him up inside. This woman with her sad eyes and lyrical voice was hard to hate. ''Not your doing.''

''Maybe so, maybe not.'' She took a step, paused and looked over her shoulder at him. ''I've got coffee up at the house. It isn't too old.'' That said, she disappeared into the brush.

He chewed another stalk of grass. He should not have

come here. The ghosts were too strong and the memories were too raw. It seemed only minutes instead of a year ago when the call came about shots fired on the old Shay ranch. Boneheaded boys taking potshots at trees had been on his mind. He never, in his darkest nightmares, envisioned finding his wife and Billy Harrigan on the banks of Crossruff Creek, shot to death with neither rhyme nor reason by Frank Shay.

They hadn't done a damned thing to deserve Shay's crazed attack. Wrong place, wrong time, wrong victims.

Breathing hard, with his heart hammering as if seeking an escape from his rib cage, he scrambled to his feet.

His life had ended when Jill's ended. The only difference was that she rested easy in the ground and he had to keep walking and breathing and suffering. He caressed the butt of the sidearm and wondered if he *was* suicidal.

He wasn't one to tolerate waste, and taking one's own life was the biggest waste of all.

He walked away from the killing ground. Grief was his cross to bear. He had to figure out a way to live with it. He reached the road where he'd parked the cruiser. A startled mourning dove whirred into the air. By squinting and knowing exactly where to look atop the mesa he could just make out the chimney on his house. Crossruff Creek originated from a spring on his property. Jill, along with Carson's best friend's teenage son, had followed the creek down the mesa to search for missing goats.

He kicked a pebble against the cruiser's tire.

He ought to accept Madeline's offer of coffee. Get inside the house, ask some questions and learn why she was *really* here. The *why* of his wife's death deviled him, always hovering at the edges of his mind, popping to the fore at every opportunity. The murders made no sense. Frank Shay made no sense. Madeline might offer a clue.

The impulse died as quickly as it had arisen. He could not stomach sitting in the house where Shay's stink permeated the walls. Besides, the state police had questioned her last year and she'd added nothing to the investigation.

He drove away, listening to the radio chatter, grateful nothing serious was happening.

He went home. From the porch he looked toward the Shay ranch. Except for power lines, the landscape. looked wild and untouched. He tried to remember if he ever saw lights or activity down there. He went inside.

Judy had left behind the scent of lemon cleansers and a plate of oatmeal cookies on the kitchen table. Bless her big heart, but whoever had told Judy Green she could cook did the world a disservice. The cookies were dust dry, hard as stone and burned on the bottoms. His freezer was full of heat-and-eat casseroles she made up. They filled the hole in his belly, but he never looked forward to eating them.

He dumped the cookies in the trash. The house seemed bigger and emptier than usual. He didn't need two hundred acres of high-country desert. He didn't need a big old farmhouse where he lacked the heart to enter half the rooms.

This had been Jill's dream home. With her funny brand of stubbornness she suffered the teasing and mock scorn of friends to raise her fancy sheep, goats and alpacas. The house haunted him with memories, but memories were all he had.

That evening he sat in the living room with the television on, unwatched, and a newspaper open on his lap, unread. He listened to the answering machine fill with cheery greetings and pleas for him to call. Voices filled with worry and concern and touches of fear. He thought again of suicide.

He was not suicidal. He wanted to be left alone.

The following morning he scrambled eggs for breakfast before heading to the barn. Rosie blew her lips in greeting. He stroked her dark neck. "Morning, old girl," he said before he opened the stall door and turned the horse out in the paddock. He filled her water trough and broke some hay flakes for her.

The mare belonged to Jill. He had sold the other horses, but Rosie was twenty-two years old and blind in one eye. He couldn't risk her ending up in a dog-food can.

He had finished up in the barn when his neighbor drove up. "Hey, big guy!" Tony Rule called and waved. Tony had removed the top and windows from his Jeep, which had oversize tires and a winch attached to the reinforced front bumper. He wore khaki shorts and a sleeveless shirt.

Carson grinned. "Back I see."

"Actually I got back day before yesterday," Tony said. "Raccoons broke into my kitchen and made a mess. I spent all day cleaning. Had to go all the way to Flagstaff to find a new screen door."

A few months ago Tony had bought the cabin and acreage at the foot of Carson's mesa. Friendly, self-absorbed and generally pleased with himself, he made a good neighbor.

"I have two cases of pale ale and a new carbide rod and reel. Got any plans this weekend?"

A few hours drowning worms might make him feel

better. Tony didn't pity him. "I'll see if I can squeeze you into my busy calendar. Where were you off to this time?"

"Toronto. That's in Canada."

Carson bit back a smirk. It amused him no end that Tony believed Carson was a country bumpkin.

"Ever thought about investing in telecommunications, big guy?"

"All that business stuff goes right over my head."

"Your loss." Tony started the Jeep. He revved the engine, making it roar. He slipped on sunglasses that probably cost more than Carson earned in a month. "See you oh-dark-thirty on Saturday."

Carson watched him drive away. He should tell Tony about Madeline Shay. Tony was an avid cross-country runner. He ran where he pleased.

Not his job, he decided. If she didn't want trespassers she should post some signs.

When he arrived at the police station, Wanda beckoned him over. She radiated excitement. A stranger sat in his office, his back to the door and his head bent toward something on his lap. Wanda snagged Carson's arm.

"You got a visitor," she whispered.

"I can see that."

"Any idea who he is?"

"I'm fixin' to find out."

"Said he's an insurance man, but he wouldn't state his business. I think he's trying to sell us something." In her book, insurance salesmen ranked below coyotes.

Carson wished Wanda would remember her job involved taking calls and handling the radios, and nothing else.

"That's interesting." The stranger turned on the chair. "I'll go see what he wants."

Wanda looked miffed at being robbed of the opportunity for self-important speculation. With a haughty sniff, she went back to her desk with its bank of radio equipment.

The insurance man stood. Carson swept off his Stetson and shook hands. The man was bespectacled and trim. His grip was timid. "Ivan Bannerman. Pleased to meet you, Chief Cody."

"Have a seat, sir." He shut the door on Wanda's prying eyes and pitcher ears. "What can I do for you today?"

He glanced at the door. "I am not a salesman, Chief Cody. I'm a claims investigator with Mutual Security and Assurance." He handed over an embossed business card.

Carson wondered why this gentleman had traveled all the way from Nevada to a little tourist town in Arizona. "If you're looking to discuss policies for the police department, you're talking to the wrong man. You need to speak to Maurice Harrigan. He's the mayor and head of the town council."

"I am not a salesman," Bannerman repeated. "I'm investigating a rather large settlement my company was forced to pay. Some new information has come to light that leads us to believe we can recover our losses."

Carson sat behind the desk. "Is that so?"

Bannerman blinked rapidly. "It concerns one of your residents. Francis Brawley Shay the Third."

The insurance man was lucky a wide desk protected him from Carson's initial impulse to strike out. He gulped down the rise of fury. "Shay is dead. I know that because I'm the one that shot him. If your company was stupid enough to insure a thug, I sure don't know what I can do for you.''

Bannerman pursed his lips.

''Shay's folks died when he was a boy. He doesn't have brothers or sisters. His widow lives on the Fort Apache reservation. Any beef you have about a settlement is with her,'' Carson said.

''If I could conduct my business without involving you, sir, I would. Quite frankly, I need your help.''

Carson tapped a pen against the desk blotter. He wished he were a rancher or a gas-station owner or a hunting guide. Any of those occupations would allow him to throw this man out the door and out of his life. As chief of police he had responsibilities—even when it felt like badgers clawed his innards.

Bannerman cleared his throat and nudged his glasses higher on his nose. ''Shay stole money from one of our clients. We settled the loss. We now believe we can recover our money.''

''I heard you guys were cracking down on fraud and theft, but this strikes me as extreme. Shay wasn't that good at robbery. I doubt he made off with more than a few thousand dollars at any one time.''

''I'm talking about millions of dollars.''

That caught his interest.

''You've heard of the Worldwide Parcel hijacking?''

Carson had to think. ''Four, five years ago. Perps hijacked an airplane and landed it in Idaho…no, Utah. What does Shay have to do with it?''

''An informant claims Shay took part in the hijacking. He hid the money before he went to prison.''

Carson ran a hand over his mouth and pulled his lower lip to prevent a bray of laughter. ''Shay got ratted out to an insurance company? Forgive me, Mr. Bannerman, but why would anyone do that?''

"Mutual Security and Assurance is offering a substantial finder's fee."

"Uh-huh."

"They got away with over thirty million dollars."

Carson stared at the little man sitting so stiffly on the tweed-covered chair. "Pardon? Did you say *thirty* million?"

"I did."

Right about then Carson could decide this was a prank, and throw this clown out of the police station. Except, a few weeks before the murders, Shay purchased a used delivery van, and outfitted it with heavy-duty tires. No one knew why a man fresh out of prison, who hadn't made a single attempt to find gainful employment, needed a delivery van.

"The state police and the sheriff's office handled the investigation. They didn't find any money."

"They weren't looking for it. Five hijackers were murdered in Utah. The rest escaped, including Shay. He stashed the money before he went to prison."

"Has your source talked to the FBI?"

"He's one of Shay's former cell mates and prefers to remain anonymous."

"I don't set much store by anonymous sources. Or jailhouse snitches."

"This one is reliable. He knows details that weren't in the newspaper or on television."

"Such as?"

"There were eight hijackers. Not even the FBI knows how many were involved."

"He could pull the number out of a hat."

"Four men boarded the plane in Las Vegas. They

had inside help from the Worldwide pilot. Four men, with two trucks waited on the ground in Utah. After the money was loaded, the leader started shooting. Shay and Deke Fry got away with the money.''

Jailhouse snitches were an inventive bunch. They had nothing but time to cook up stories.

Tightness gripped Carson's chest and climbed his throat. Until a year ago he had never thought of himself as a vengeful man. A year ago he rose from bed each morning eager to go to work. He no longer cared about anything except finding a way to make things right. Bannerman offered the possibility of answers. If he could figure out why Shay had murdered his wife, he would feel better.

''Interesting details, Mr. Bannerman, but he could be jerking your chain.''

''Considering how much money is at stake, I'm willing to take the chance.''

Carson scribbled ''Deke Fry'' on his desk blotter.

''Shay and Fry hid the money until the heat was off. Shay got into a bar fight and was arrested. Jail turned out to be a good place to hide. Fry disappeared.''

''You've looked for him?''

''I most certainly have.''

''Fry recovered the money when Shay got locked up,'' Carson said.

''Shay was too smart.''

Carson doubted it. ''What about the third man? The leader. Name?''

Bannerman picked at his trouser leg. ''No one knows. He's a master criminal. He recruited the hijackers, turned the pilot, planned the entire heist and killed the witnesses. Shay was supposed to die in Utah like all the others.''

"Did you give this information to the FBI?"

Bannerman pulled off the glasses and blew lightly on the lenses. "The FBI has been less than cooperative with Mutual Security and Assurance. They demand the name of my source."

"Sounds reasonable."

"If I knew his name. I've only spoken to him by telephone and he demands anonymity."

Carson sensed a lie. "How can he collect a reward?"

"We have procedures to reward anonymous tips."

"I don't know how I can help you, sir. The hijacking is the fed's case."

"I read about what happened to you, Chief Cody. My condolences for your loss."

Carson lowered his eyelids and leaned back on the chair.

"While money is a paltry substitute for a loved one, it can help ease the pain." He watched Carson as if judging the effect of his words. "I would like your help—Mutual Security and Assurance would like your help in recovering the money."

"Need a shovel?"

Bannerman wrinkled his face. "It is Mutual Security and Assurance's policy to obtain official sanction for our investigations. I need someone who is familiar with this area. I also need the assurance of privacy. People get rather…excited when it comes to large sums of money."

"You want me to help you dig up the Shay ranch and not tell anybody why." Carson nodded as if it made sense. He damned himself for being interested.

"The finder's fee is considerable."

"I work for the town, not for rewards."

Bannerman flinched. "It's not my intent to insult you."

He wondered if Madeline knew about a truckload of cash. "I need to do some fact checking before I make a decision."

"I do hope you'll be discreet. If this leaks to the media it could turn ugly real fast."

Now Carson was insulted. "You have my word. I won't tell anybody anything until I've discussed it with you."

"Mutual Security and Assurance did not suffer lightly having to pay thirty million dollars to World-wide. We have to answer to our shareholders."

"There is one small problem."

"What's that?"

"The Shay ranch is private property. You'll need the owner's permission to search."

Bannerman seemed stunned. "I thought the property was vacant."

"Shay's daughter lives there."

A sneaking suspicion said Madeline Shay wouldn't cooperate with the man who killed her father.

Chapter Two

Madeline rubbed grit from her eyes. She arched her back and rolled her shoulders, working out the kinks. She needed a good work light, but the utility company demanded a deposit before turning on the electricity. Not that this was too horrible. April in northern Arizona meant plenty of sunshine. The garage made a good natural-light studio. She had plenty of peace and quiet.

Maybe a tad too much isolation. All her life, she had wished for a hermit's cave, away from phones, television, radio and people. Perfect silence in which to think and create.

Now that she had it, it sucked. She missed Uncle Willy and her little cousins. She missed talking to customers at the trading post. She longed to call Nona Redhawk to talk about art.

She stood and stretched, and walked outside. The garage was in better shape than the house, and it smelled better, too. The concrete floor was smooth, the walls were sturdy and in plumb. On the metal exterior walls, beneath the vile graffiti, lay a fairly fresh coat of paint.

The mesa towering to the east drew her gaze and thoughts to Carson Cody. Spotting his cruiser on the road had scared her, but seeing him had filled her with pity. He gave new meaning to despair and sorrow.

She wondered what he would do if she took him a gift. Throw it in her face? Nothing could ever make up for what her father had done.

Sighing, she carried her work-in-progress to the doorway to examine it in full sun. She armed sweat off her brow. While working, she didn't notice the heat. Covering a tall wooden vessel in seed beads was a painstaking process. She used gourd stitch, sewing on beads one at a time. A phoenix pattern emerged, the dark bird rising from the flames. She dampened childish delight in the pattern and colors and the hypnotic brilliance of the tiny glass beads, and turned on her critical eye. She had learned the craft from bead workers who had learned from their ancestors. Living up to the knowledge they imparted so generously demanded brutal honesty about her efforts. She searched for buckling caused by odd-sized beads, for gaps in the increases and decreases, and for mistakes in the pattern. She discovered a black bead where a red bead should be.

An approaching vehicle caught her attention. Dust rose over the scrub. Her one visit to Ruff a year ago had left a nasty taste in her mouth. She'd been threatened with violence that transcended reason. That they were capable of it was evident in the house and garage. They were covered with filthy words and curses. Every window in the house was broken and holes were shot through the roof. People had left behind mounds of beer cans and other trash. Vandals had left something especially nasty beneath the house and sometimes the smell grew so bad she took her sleeping bag to the garage. Fortunately, the well was good. The rusty old hand pump was a pain to operate, but at least she had clean water.

At the sight of a police cruiser, she relaxed. Carson Cody might hate her, but their brief encounter had proved him a decent man. A sad, heavyhearted man, but decent nonetheless.

The cruiser pulled up to the house. Madeline sneezed. She groaned at the thought of all that dust settling on her worktable. Chief Cody parked behind her van. His broad-brimmed cowboy hat shadowed his face. Another man exited the cruiser.

Hiding fear and nervousness were second nature to Madeline. Head up and shoulders straight, she walked across the barren yard. "May I help you?"

The police chief tipped his hat. He was a big man with broad, muscular shoulders and long limbs. If he had a decent haircut and a facial, he'd make a good model for advertising pickup trucks. The other man wore a suit. He looked around as if expecting something to bite him.

"Miss Shay," Carson said, "sorry to bother you. This is Ivan Bannerman, of Mutual Security and Assurance. An insurance company. He hopes you can help him with a problem."

She looked at the insurance man then back at the trashed house. The attorney representing her father's estate had found her easily enough. She couldn't imagine why it had taken the insurance company so long. "What's this all about?"

Bannerman was a quivering little ferret. "Please excuse our interruption, but I'm sure you'll understand how important this is." He fanned his face with a hand. "Whew, it sure is hot out here."

She folded her arms.

His tremulous smile faded. "I'm a claims investigator for Mutual Security and Assurance. A criminal action against one of our corporate clients caused our company a substantial loss. We have reason to believe it may be possible to recoup that loss." His speech sounded rehearsed.

Madeline didn't have time to play. "When you refer to a criminal action, you're talking about my father, right?" She slid a look at Carson. Sunglasses concealed his thoughts. "If you're hoping to recoup your losses from his estate, you're out of luck. This ranch is worthless."

Bannerman squared his shoulders. "It's not the land. It's what might be buried on it. I would like permission to search."

Her scalp and neck prickled. Carson Cody had no right to parade strangers around on her land. "What is this really about? I told you I don't want trouble. I haven't set foot in your town and I won't. So leave me alone."

He pulled off the sunglasses and hooked them in the front of his uniform shirt. "Excuse me, Mr. Bannerman, I'd like a word in private with Miss Shay."

The little man bristled like an offended rooster. "We agreed—"

"I know what we agreed. A moment."

Carson walked toward the garage. Madeline looked warily between the men.

"I sort of thought we had a deal," she said. "I don't bother you and you don't bother me."

"This isn't harassment," he said. "Mr. Bannerman has some ideas about why your father did what he did."

She had twelve more pieces to finish for the autumn art show in Santa Fe. A successful showing and sales meant the financial freedom to rent a proper studio. It meant commissions and interest from galleries. Failure meant having to take yet more menial jobs that left her too exhausted for art.

"I know how much you hate my father and what he did. I know it's too much to ask that you put it behind you. Trust me, Chief Cody, if I had somewhere else to go, I'd go there. I only need a few months. That's all, I promise. Then you'll never have to think about me again."

He turned a frown on his boots. "This isn't about you."

Meeting him at the creek and now his showing up with a stranger could not be a coincidence.

"Anything worth searching for was stolen or smashed up already." She indicated the house with a slash of her hand.

He didn't react.

Maybe she should beg Uncle Willy for a place to stay. He and Aunt Alma had six kids, three under the age of four, and his wife's mother lived with them, crammed into a tiny house. She'd never get any work done.

For the cops to run her off when she hadn't hurt anyone or broken any laws was unfair.

He removed his hat and held it over his chest. His eyes were gray, as pale as moonlight in his sun-darkened face. In them lay compassion, perhaps even apology. He was easy on the eyes, and for some odd reason it made her angrier. It was as if he used his attractiveness as a weapon. Which was ridiculous, but it floated through her head anyway.

"It's not my intention to run roughshod over you."

She huffed a sarcastic laugh. "You sure didn't waste any time blowing my cover."

"You asked me why he did it. If you allow Mr. Bannerman to search the ranch, we might dig up some answers."

She pointed her chin at the dilapidated house. "The old serve and protect? Where were you when my tires got slashed in broad daylight, right in front of the funeral home? Who were you protecting when creeps trashed the house? Gee, Mr. Policeman, why don't you put up a billboard to let everyone know I'm here?"

His face darkened. A muscle jumped in his jaw and those pale eyes turned to glass. He settled the hat back on his head. "If you cooperate, I'll see you and your property are protected."

"If I don't? You stand by while the rednecks lynch me?"

"I meant, after a look around, we'll leave you be. You don't have to worry about anyone else bothering you."

Maintaining anger in the face of so much sincerity was difficult. She jammed her hands into her back pockets and scraped the dirt with the toe of her sandal. "What is he looking for?"

He slid a hand across his nape. "He doesn't want anyone to know. It's, uh, sensitive."

"Right."

"It's for your own protection, Miss Shay."

"This is ridiculous. Take that so-called insurance salesman and get off my land."

"Talk to—"

He suddenly turned to face the road beyond the cruiser. A fresh dust cloud formed and within seconds he heard the growl of an engine. He walked fast across the yard. When a pickup truck came into view, Carson blocked its way. He thrust out a hand, ordering the driver to stop.

Bannerman pushed away from the cruiser. His mouth hung open.

Madeline mentally screamed at them to go away. Anger sat ill with her, especially since she didn't want to be angry with Carson Cody. His sorrow haunted her. His action today struck her as the worst sort of betrayal. It was as if he didn't have the guts to order her outright to get out of town. He had to come in here with a lame excuse to search for *something*. And now more intruders had arrived.

The pickup's driver opened the door, but Carson ordered him to stay inside. There were two men in the truck. Madeline inched inside the garage. The police chief's voice rose in anger.

"I said, turn around and git! Stay off this land. It's none of your concern."

The engine roared. Madeline feared he'd accelerate right past the police chief and run her down. Gears screamed and the driver backed up. Dust and brush swallowed the truck.

"Miss Shay," Bannerman said, walking toward her. "I apologize for Chief Cody—"

"Do you think I don't know what you're up to? I own this land! I have every right to be here. You are not going to run me off!"

"Miss Shay—"

She wished for a door to slam in his face. She didn't have one, so she sat on a stool, with her back to him. She didn't breathe easier until she heard the cruiser's engine start. She didn't turn around until the sound of tires crunching gravel had faded away.

She didn't cry, she never cried, though she was as close to it as she had been in years. This land was hers, damn it. No small-town cop, no matter how big a grudge he carried, could run her off.

CARSON LOOKED both ways on the road, seeking any sign of Matt Harrigan's pickup truck. Of all the people to get a bad case of nosiness, it had to be Matt and Sug Harrigan. Frank Shay had murdered their cousin. Seeing Madeline Shay was guaranteed to drive them crazy.

"What happened back there?" Bannerman sounded squeaky. "Who are those men? What do they want? You didn't tell anybody about the money, did you?"

Grimacing, Carson drew his head aside. "Calm down. Those are local ranchers. Being nosy." He worked his jaw against the tightness. With any luck, the brothers hadn't recognized Madeline. It wasn't unusual for campers and hikers to set up camp on private land. "I'm sorry, sir. As I explained, without express consent, you can't trespass on her land."

"Thirty million dollars!"

Carson shrugged. "Tell her the truth."

"She'll look for it on her own."

Better Madeline earn the finder's fee than some jail-bird.

"There must be some legal maneuver you can use," Bannerman said.

Civilians.

Even if Carson knew a way to bend the law, he wouldn't do it. He wasn't that kind of cop and didn't intend to become one.

"If she suddenly starts throwing thirty million bucks around, then I'm sure your company can stake a claim to it." He hoped the Harrigan boys weren't waiting for him to leave.

"We're talking about a major crime here, Chief Cody. Hijacking, robbery, murder. Surely you—"

"So you say, based on the word of a crook," Carson interrupted. "I don't discount your job. I don't deny my personal interest, either. But the only way I can search her property against her wishes is with a warrant."

Bannerman slouched on the seat and stared at the passing landscape.

Carson guessed the insurance man didn't like hearing the word no. He'd better get used to it. Madeline Shay was one stubborn, gutsy woman. His uniform didn't intimidate her and neither did Bannerman.

Her sharp words stung, but he didn't blame her. The condition of the old house had shocked him. Every window busted, holes punched in the walls, and graffiti obscene enough to shock a sailor. He could only imagine what the house looked like on the inside.

"She knows about the money."

Carson glanced at Bannerman. "Excuse me?"

"She knows about the money. That's why she won't let me look."

"If that's what thirty million buys, what's the point of having it?"

"Shay talked about her all the time." Bannerman sounded as if that were stone-cold fact rather than the chatter of a jailhouse snitch. "He told her about the money."

The road rose into the rocky hills and the vegetation changed from scrub to pine trees. Ruff used to be made up of ranchers and hunters. Now tourism was the leading industry. The feed store carried souvenirs and camping supplies. Cafés offered lattes and espresso. The town boasted two national motel chains and six fast-food restaurants. Out of habit, Carson scanned automobiles, sorting locals from the tourists. He drove behind the courthouse, which contained the magistrate's chamber, health department, clerk-recorder, police station, and public library.

He parked in the spot marked Chief of Police. "I appreciate your dilemma, sir. Wish I had a solution for you."

"Are you prepared for a gold rush if word gets out about the money?" Bannerman pushed open the car door. "I don't think you are."

The insurance man stomped across the parking lot to his rental car. Wondering if the little pissant had threatened him, Carson went inside.

He went straight to his office and shut the door. The tourist season was kicking into gear, causing an influx of petty crimes. His in-box was filled with reports, the majority involving traffic violations.

An unmistakable voice boomed through the closed door. Maurice Harrigan, Ruff's mayor, insisted on seeing the chief.

Carson braced for the storm.

Maurice shoved into the office. "Damn you! Why didn't you tell me that half-breed was in my town?"

Matt and Sug jostled through the doorway. Matt was a few inches taller than his younger brother, but otherwise they looked like twins. Towheaded, ruddy faced and stocky, the nephews folded their brawny arms over their brawny chests, doing their best to look menacing.

"Last I looked," Carson said, "you only own about half the town, not the whole of it."

"Don't give me your lip." Maurice dropped onto a

chair. "The boys saw that half-breed with their own eyes. You were being nice and cozy with her."

By Carson's reckoning, the entire town would know of her presence by sunset. "Madeline Shay has every right to be there."

"Her daddy killed my boy. She's got no right at all to flaunt that in my face!"

Carson had known Maurice since boyhood. As a kid, Maurice had been class president, star athlete and all-round mover-and-shaker. A more energetic, civic-minded, generous man couldn't be found in the entire state. Carson used to consider Maurice his best friend.

Used to... Maurice had never said it straight out, but he blamed Jill for Billy's murder. If not for her lost goats, Billy would be alive. They barely spoke these days.

"Boys," Carson said to the nephews, "mind giving me and your uncle a moment?"

Neither made a move until Maurice nodded curtly. The young men trooped out and Sug slammed the door.

"I know how you feel. The mere sight of her puts an arrow in my heart. But she's a private citizen and the land legally belongs to her."

"It's not right. You have to do something."

"She isn't coming into town. No intention of bothering anybody. She's working on a project that will take a few weeks. Then she'll be gone."

"It's a slap in the face to the entire community. Shoot, Carson, she's barely a rock skip from your front porch. How can you stand knowing she's there?"

"Her daddy did the damage, not her. If we're going to get all caught up in the sins of the father, then what about the virtues of her grandfather? Pat and Lois Shay were good people. Good citizens."

Color seeped from Maurice's face, leaving him gray. He looked eighty years old. "It doesn't go away. Every morning I wake up thinking, okay, it won't hurt so bad today. Only it does. I still have the girls. Still have Mary. They can't make up for losing Billy."

"I know."

"Why can't that girl go back to the reservation? It's better for everybody all the way around. Safer, too. Frank Shay wasn't popular with anybody."

Carson rested his arms on the desk and stared until Maurice met his eyes. "You're a good man, a good mayor. You've got three daughters and a wife to see to. Businesses to run, a ranch to manage. Don't let Frank Shay take that away from you, too."

"I'm not making threats."

Carson arched a brow. "I know you too well. You're not saying the words, but I know what you're thinking."

"You're thinking it, too."

"You'd lose a bet on that. Leave her alone."

"It's not right...."

"I looked it up. Madeline Shay paid the tax bill in full two months ago. Deed is in her name. So put her out of mind. I guarantee she won't step foot in town."

Maurice released a heavy sigh. He had lost a lot of weight in the past year. His shirt collar gapped and his gold wedding ring shifted loose on his finger. His auburn hair had faded to ginger and receded dramatically from his forehead. He was Carson's age, not quite forty, but he looked ancient. Carson wondered if he looked as tired and trail worn as Maurice.

"Tell your nephews if anything happens, I'll look to them first. I won't treat it like their usual shenanigans, either."

Maurice rose. "Yeah, yeah, straight and narrow. You're the only cop I know who'd give his boss a ticket."

"You were speeding." He grinned, recalling the incident.

Maurice returned a faint smile. "Have it your way then. Can't blame that Indian girl for what her no-good daddy did. Just make sure she stays out of town. I can't be responsible for everybody."

Carson didn't know whether to trust him or not.

Pete Morales poked his head inside the office. The sergeant's normally placid face was a study in worry. "Is it true? Madeline Shay is living at her father's place?"

So much for Madeline keeping a low profile. He rubbed his weary eyes.

"How do you feel about it, Chief?"

He wished people would quit worrying about his damned feelings. "She can live where she likes. Do me a favor, Pete. Put out the word, any officer who uses a badge to harass Miss Shay faces suspension. Now go on out and shut the door. I have things to do."

Pete looked as if he had plenty more to say. He backed out of the office.

Carson looked up a number. He called the northern office of the Arizona State Police and asked for Lieutenant Paul Imagia.

"Imagia."

"Paul, this is Carson Cody, over in Ruff."

"Hey! How are you doing, man?" The lieutenant was in his fifties, but on the telephone he sounded like a college frat boy.

"Do you have a few minutes to talk?"

"For you? I have nothing but time. What do you need?"

"You took part in the manhunt after the Worldwide Parcel hijacking and robbery, right?"

"Like almost everybody else in the Four Corners area. That was years ago."

"Was the money ever recovered?"

"Not a penny. Why?"

"Do you know if Frank Shay was ever connected to the hijacking?"

A long silence greeted the question and Carson wondered if the connection had been lost.

"That's an odd thing to ask," Paul finally said.

"I heard a rumor Shay was one of the hijackers. Is it possible?"

"It's possible the president of the United States is one of the hijackers, but not likely. Far as I know there aren't any viable suspects. The case is cold as ice. I haven't heard mention of it in years."

"Could you ask around? Talk to your contacts in the FBI?"

"What the hell kind of rumor did you hear?"

"One of those little whispers that sounds crazy enough to be true."

"I'll ask," Paul said. "Only because you want me to. Not because I think it'll go anywhere."

"Thanks. I appreciate it."

An idea occurred to him, but it was a nutty idea and he shoved it from mind. He ignored it the rest of the day, but on the way home it returned with a vengeance. He stood on the front porch and looked toward the Shay ranch.

The way Madeline lived appalled him. No electricity, no running water and having to stare day after day at the venomous graffiti covering the ruins of the old ranch house.

Inside he slid one of Judy's atrocious casseroles into the oven. He kept seeing Madeline face him down, her Madonna face carved from marble, her green eyes steady. If not for him, her presence would still be a secret.

While he changed clothes, tended Rosie and choked down a yellow concoction that was either tuna casserole or chicken à la king, he mulled over whether or not Madeline knew about the money. If she did know, why wait an entire year to go looking for it?

Bannerman had wrested a promise from Carson to keep quiet about the money. He could talk to Madeline about other matters. A conversation might turn naturally to her father and his criminal activities. If she recovered the money, it didn't matter to Mutual Security and Assurance who collected the finder's fee.

He picked up the truck keys. They were neighbors after all. A friendly visit should prove he wasn't a hard-ass cop trying to run her off.

He bypassed the cruiser and climbed into his pickup. Bannerman could go to hell. Carson's primary duty was keeping the peace, and that overrode the fiscal problems of an out-of-state insurance company.

While he drove off the mesa, he practiced what to say. He didn't know how to act around an angry woman, or most women in general, for that matter. Not a man living intimidated him, but females? A pretty smile or the threat of tears took him to his knees.

A glow over the trees puzzled him. Tony Rule's cabin, the closest neighbor with electricity, lay in another direction. He had driven about a hundred yards before he realized what he looked at. Fire.

He punched the accelerator. A vehicle barreled out of the entrance to the Shay ranch, heading fast toward town.

It was too far away. He couldn't make out the model, color or license plate. Instinct urged him to give chase, but the fire was more important.

It burned on Madeline's land.

Chapter Three

Headlights bounced off the scrub lining the ranch drive-way. The sky above glowed orange, shot through with billows of smoke. Carson felt as if he drove in slow motion, that the driveway was a hundred miles long and he'd never reach Madeline in time.

He grabbed for the radio mike before remembering he was in the truck. He fumbled at his belt, shirt pocket and passenger seat even though a sick feeling said his cell phone was sitting on the kitchen table where he'd emptied out his pockets.

He broke from the trees and his heart hit his gut with a thud.

The house was engulfed. Fire crackled and swirled around blackened timbers. He killed the truck engine and pushed open the door. Heat slapped his face and his eyes stung. The fire roared like a tornado. A hot hail of cinders pelted his hat and arms. He turned the truck so it faced away from the fire in case the surrounding scrub caught fire and he had to escape. He grabbed the large flashlight out of the holder attached to the dash-board.

"Madeline!" he yelled.

Firelight cast weird, shifting shadows. A smaller fire

burned a few yards from the house. Glass shattered. A van burned almost as ferociously as the house. He pressed a forearm over his brow, shielding his eyes from the heat. A stench of gasoline mingled with smoke.

"Madeline!" He ran toward the house.

Scorching heat shoved him back.

He ran around the perimeter, seeking any sign of life, any way past the wall of flame. The garage was untouched. The sliding door was open enough for a slim body to slip through. Shouting for Madeline, hoping against hope, he shoved the door and turned on the flashlight. So much dust and smoke swirled inside the garage that he wondered if he'd made a mistake and it was on fire after all. Smoke particles diffused and muted the light.

A faint groan made him freeze. He strained to hear beyond the whoosh and roar of the flaming house. He heard it again. He scuttled forward, bent over while holding his shirt collar over his mouth. He shone the flashlight along the floor and into the corners.

He found her curled in a tight ball beneath a table. She moaned painfully and coughed. The smoke and heat increased. He checked the path to the door then shoved the flashlight into his belt. He gathered Madeline into his arms. Her groans turned into whimpers as he hurried out of the garage. Every breath was like trying to swallow sandpaper. Gusts of hot wind swirled. The roof collapsed sending up a cloud of sparks and snapping embers. Carson lugged Madeline to the truck. He had to lower her legs so he could get the door opened. She nearly slithered from his grasp.

"Get in," he urged her. "Come on, work with me. Get in." He pushed her inside. She was covered in soot, dirt and blood. All she wore was an oversize T-shirt.

"Can you talk to me? Madeline, come on, can you talk?"

She pushed hair off her face. The gesture seemed to take all her strength. Her lips were split. Blood trickled from a cut on her forehead.

The van's gas tank exploded.

An enormous *whump* accompanied a hot hand shoving Carson against the open truck door. His eardrums pulsed. He dropped to one knee and instinctively shielded his head with both arms. He waited for shrapnel to tear through his body. He grew dizzy from holding his breath before he knew they were in the clear. He rose and looked back.

The van was a fireball.

Someone should have noticed the flames by now and alerted the fire department.

A touch on his shoulder startled him. Madeline's mouth moved, but he couldn't understand her. He wondered if she'd lost her teeth or broken her jaw. Then it hit him that it wasn't the roar of the fire he heard, but buzzing inside his head. He worked his jaw to pop his ears and shook his head.

"Strap yourself in." He barely heard his own voice.

Of all the nights to forget his cell phone. Cursing his own stupidity, he ran around the front of the truck. He tore the flashlight from his belt and flung it onto the seat before he slid behind the wheel. The rearview mirror blazed orange with reflected flames.

At the road he searched for approaching fire trucks. Madeline was sitting up straight and seemed to be breathing normally. Her mouth formed the words, "I'm okay."

Tony Rule's cabin was closer than Carson's house.

Tony would have a first-aid kit and a telephone. Carson headed there.

Lights were on and as soon as Carson pulled up, Tony appeared in the doorway. Carson jumped out of the truck.

Tony yelled, "Hey, don't you know the cops are death on speeders around here?"

"I need some help," Carson yelled back. "I've got an injured woman."

Tony helped Carson unload Madeline and carry her into the house. They placed her on a leather sofa. "I'll be right back," Tony said, and hurried out of the room.

Carson crouched next to Madeline and stroked blood-crusted hair from her face. Her eyes were wide and scared.

"I'm okay," she said, her voice cracked and husky. "I don't think I'm hurt."

It sounded like a wasp's nest in his head, but Carson heard her clearly.

"What happened?" Tony asked. He draped a blanket over Madeline. He wrinkled his nose and looked between them, his expression worried. "No offense, but you guys stink."

"Take a gander out your back door. I need your phone."

"Kitchen." Tony led the way. The fire was visible through the window. "Is that a forest fire?" Tony exclaimed in horror.

"Not yet." Carson knocked the side of his head with his palm in a vain attempt to dislodge the ringing.

He called the fire station. The fire chief, Dooley Duran answered. It was poker night for the volunteers and men were laughing in the background. "Break off the game, Dooley, there's a fire out at the Shay ranch."

"Carson?" Dooley said.

"Yes, it's Carson. There's a fire."

"Did you say the Shay ranch?"

"Out on Hoshonee Road. The house is on fire and a vehicle exploded. I need EMTs, too. I've got an injured woman."

"The Indian girl? Life-threatening injuries?"

Carson answered, "I don't think so," and knew it was a mistake as soon as he spoke.

"Are you there now?" Dooley sounded bored.

Carson wanted to reach through the phone and grab Dooley by the throat. "I'm at Tony Rule's cabin, the old Gonzales place. Get a move on before we have a wildfire on our hands."

"Okeydoke." Dooley hung up.

Carson glared at the handset before slamming the phone onto the cradle. Dooley and the rest of the firefighters better do their jobs no matter how they felt about Madeline Shay.

His friend raked both hands through his shock of black hair. "It looks huge. Who's the pretty lady?"

"Grab a first-aid kit and a towel." He called Pete Morales at home. When the sergeant answered, Carson explained the situation. He trusted Pete to do his job and do it well no matter who was the victim. He returned to the front room.

Tony stood by with a white box marked with a red cross, and a dampened towel slung over one wrist. Madeline was sitting up. She'd wrapped the blanket around her shoulders. Her bare legs and feet were streaked with soot and dirt. Carson gently tipped her face in order to examine the cut on her forehead.

"Ambulance is on the way," he said.

"No ambulance." She coughed and grimaced as if it hurt.

"You swallowed smoke. You need a doctor to check you out."

"I can't pay for it. Forget it. I'm okay."

"Don't worry about the money."

"Easy for you to say." She swiped her eyes with the back of her hand and coughed again.

Carson used the damp towel to wipe blood and soot off her face. She flinched. The cuts on her forehead and lip were minor. He squirted a dab of antibiotic cream on the forehead cut and covered it with a bandage. She coughed. When he asked if it hurt her chest, she denied it.

Tony handed Madeline a glass of ice water. She thanked him and drank greedily. Water dribbled down her chin. She winced with every swallow. Tony offered Carson a beer. He shook his head in refusal, and went to the front door, where he searched the darkness for approaching emergency vehicles.

He would figure out who had fled the scene. Arson, assault and battery—someone was going to jail. He had a fairly good idea that someone was a towheaded hot-head who answered to Harrigan.

"Do I get an introduction?" Tony asked.

To hear Tony talk, women fell all over him and he had lady friends in every city he visited. His wolfish grin said he wouldn't mind adding Madeline to his list of conquests.

Under normal circumstances, Tony's self-centered arrogance amused Carson. Right now his friend seemed callous and predatory.

"Give us a moment in private," Carson said. "Police business."

Tony's eyes darted from Carson to Madeline then back again. Smiling, he shrugged. "I'll make a pot of coffee. I have some Kenyan beans that'll knock your socks off."

Taking care not to jostle Madeline, Carson sat on the sofa. Her facial injuries fueled his temper. In his book, men who abused women were lower than scorpions and deserved the same treatment. "Who hit you, Madeline?"

"Nobody. I don't know. I was sleeping." She touched a finger to her split lip and winced. "It's all a blur. All I remember is the fire and getting out the window." A lone tear trickled down her dirty cheek. "It was so hot and smoky. I couldn't see. I put up a board to keep out the bugs. I must have broken it. I got out. I hid. I tried to hide." She drew in a long, ragged breath. "I don't know what happened."

Carson's gorge rose. The bastard had left her to burn.

MADELINE SIPPED a second glass full of ice water. The shock subsided. She tested her teeth with her tongue, not quite daring to believe they were all there. She remembered getting tangled in the sleeping bag and falling on her face. Her throat felt as if a rough hand had worked over her esophagus with steel wool.

She cocked her head to listen to men talking in the kitchen. A cop in uniform had arrived a few minutes ago.

"Can I get you anything else?"

She lifted her gaze to Tony. He was as tall as Carson, but had the tight, lean build of a marathon runner. He was almost pretty with black hair, very blue eyes surrounded by a thick fringe of lashes, a perfectly straight nose and a full lower lip. He wore baggy shorts and a tank top that showed off his muscular arms. He smiled, his interest open and unabashed.

She tugged the blanket tighter around her shoulders. "I'm fine. Thank you."

He waited for her to introduce herself. Carson had ignored requests by Tony to introduce them. She hesitated, uncertain how he'd react to allowing her in his house.

"I'm Tony Rule, resident layabout." He thrust out his right hand. His grip was warm and gentle.

"I'm Madeline. Thank you for helping me."

"I can't resist a damsel in distress. Were you and Carson...camping?"

She shook her head. She eyed the pelts, hides and animal heads hanging on the walls. Deer, elk, moose and javelina stared through glass eyes. Madeline had nothing against responsible hunters, but trophies gave her the creeps.

He pointed down a hallway. "If you want to clean up or something, the bathroom is that way."

Feeling naked and exposed in the old T-shirt she wore as pajamas she held on to the blanket.

Behind the bathroom door, she allowed a few tears to fall. Her emotions were divided so strongly they may as well have been sitting on her shoulders playing angel and devil. The devil stridently accused Carson of telling everyone she was in the area; the angel regarded him with adoration for saving her life.

She sucked in a deep breath. Her lungs ached. Swallowing hurt. She stopped shaking. With steady hands she turned on the water tap. Her reflection was hollow eyed and filthy. The rank smell of smoke gagged her. She washed her face, hands and arms, but her hair reeked of smoke. She eyed the shower stall and sighed. She could not impose that much.

When she left the bathroom, Carson and the other cop were in the front room, along with a pair of young men wearing emergency services shirts.

"No ambulance," she said. She pleaded with her eyes for Carson to understand. "I'm fine."

"Let them check you out." Carson beckoned with his hand.

The shorter of the EMTs picked up a medical case. He leveled a contemptuous gaze on Madeline. "Hey, if she don't want help I won't force her."

The other EMT looked confused and made a motion to take the case from his partner.

"That's Frank Shay's daughter," the first one said, and walked out the door. Understanding dawned on the other's face.

Madeline lifted her chin, refusing to let them see her humiliation. "I do not need any help. Thank you very much."

The EMT turned for the door, but Carson blocked the way. He looked taller, bigger, his shoulders bunched up and his head lowered. Those gray eyes burned with dangerous light. The EMT backed away and drew his hands to his chest.

"You do not pick and choose who to help," Carson said. "Do your job."

"I, uh—"

"Let him go," Madeline said. "I don't want help."

Carson allowed the EMT to escape. "I'll run you down to the clinic in Whiteriver."

Better he turned her out naked in the middle of Ruff rather than returning to Whiteriver. "I'm fine."

His face was streaked with soot and his hands were

filthy. He had saved her life. One word from her and he'd drag those EMTs by the collars back into the house. The devil voice faded.

"I am truly fine," she said more calmly. She looked at the other cop and Tony. He stared as if she'd sprouted a third eye in the middle of her forehead. "I'm more shaken than hurt."

Carson rubbed the back of his neck and glowered at the floor. "I need you to give Sergeant Morales a statement. Tony, we can take this elsewhere and get out of your hair."

"*Mi casa, su casa,* big guy. I'm more than happy to help." He chuckled. "Even if I do have to keep leaving the room. Banished like a naughty child." With a comical roll of his eyes, he sauntered into the kitchen.

Okay then, Madeline thought, maybe Tony didn't realize who she was.

Sergeant Morales pulled a chair to face the sofa. He was Hispanic and his eyes were dark and wise. "Are you really okay?"

She couldn't tell from his voice or expression if he was sincere. She lifted a shoulder.

Carson remained by the front door. He watched the night, but she sensed he paid attention to her.

Sergeant Morales asked, "Are you up to telling me what happened?" He held a pen and notebook.

"I don't quite know what happened. I was asleep. Then the house was on fire."

"Your face didn't get like that by going through the window," Carson said without turning around.

She touched her tongue to her swollen lower lip. "I fell. My feet got caught in the sleeping bag and I fell on my face."

"I saw a vehicle fleeing the scene. Did you see anybody? Did anybody touch you?"

"I'm asking the questions, Chief," Morales said while he wrote. "Did you see anybody, Miss Shay?"

Madeline forced her memory into gear. Try as she might, the only thing she remembered was the smoke and the heat and scrambling out the window. "No, I did not."

"Any ideas about the vehicle, Chief?"

"I saw it exit the driveway onto Hoshonee Road, but I was too far away to see more than headlights. I'm pretty sure the driver saw my car approach."

Morales grunted. "Mind if I take a few pictures to document your injuries?"

She looked again at Carson. "Why?"

Carson finally turned around. His mouth was set in a grim line. "This is going to court, Madeline. I will catch the responsible party."

In another place, another time, she might have believed him. This was Ruff, and her father's crimes were too fresh. Not even the paramedics could overcome their revulsion. "You'll never catch them. You'll never prove anything."

Carson and Morales exchanged a look. "We're small-town folk," Morales said. "But we're good cops. Arson is serious business."

"Like you said, Chief Cody, Ruff isn't a healthy place for me. Guess I should have listened." She tightened the blanket around her shoulders and wished they would leave her in peace.

"Damn right you should have," he said. Color rose in his face.

His sharp tone made her stiffen. Even Morales looked surprised.

Carson's boots rocked the floor. "Pete, document her injuries. Tony? Do you have a phone where I can speak privately?"

Tony appeared in the doorway. "My bedroom. End of the hallway."

Carson stalked away. Madeline could feel the vibration of his anger trailing him like a wake. Her indignation rose. If anyone had cause for anger, she did. Carson Cody should be ashamed of himself.

"Take your pictures," she said.

In silence she allowed the police sergeant to photograph her face and her hands where she had scraped them in her escape from the burning house. The sergeant was gentle with her, but she sank inside her mind. He was one of them, one of the enemy. She, who had felt the outsider all her life, had never felt so alone.

SERGEANT MORALES FINISHED taking her statement and left. Carson rattled car keys, ready to go.

"You are more than welcome to stay here tonight," Tony said. "I'd love the company."

The mere thought of trying to sleep under those dead animals was too depressing to think about. But Madeline had nowhere else to go.

"She needs police protection," Carson said. "She's coming with me."

She supposed spending the night in a jail cell was better than worrying about another fire.

Tony spread his arms. "I'm armed to the teeth, big guy. I'll protect this beautiful lady with my life."

Madeline knew he joked, trying to add a little levity, but it fell flat. She chewed silently on the annoyance until certain her voice wouldn't betray her feelings. "I appreciate all you've done, Mr. Rule. I'd better go with

Chief Cody.'' She rose. She tightened her hold on the blanket, unwilling to release it. Her T-shirt was thin, ragged and full of holes. She hoped they had clothes for her at the jail.

''Ah, come on. Look at her, she's exhausted,'' Tony said. ''Let her stay.''

He was too eager. His eyes were too bold and his smile was too big. Her defenses were too low to deal with a man like him. ''Thank you for the blanket.'' She lowered it slowly, hoping he offered to let her keep it. Tony followed the blanket's progress with open interest.

''Keep the blanket,'' Carson said, shifting impatiently from foot to foot. ''I don't need you taking a chill and coming down with pneumonia. Thanks for everything, man. I'll talk to you tomorrow.'' He held the door and Madeline hurried outside.

''You need to see a doctor.'' Carson opened the truck door for her. ''Smoke inhalation can make you sick.''

She couldn't afford to get sick, but she couldn't afford a doctor bill, either. She had the money she needed until the Santa Fe show and not a penny more. She climbed inside the truck. He shut the door.

When he started driving, she said, ''I've never been in jail before.''

He slid a puzzled look at her. ''Good to know.''

He turned onto the road leading up the mesa. She mulled it over in her increasingly foggy brain before realizing they weren't going to town. ''Aren't you putting me in jail?''

''Why would I do that?''

''Police protection.''

''I am the police. I apologize for Tony, by the way. He's a good guy even if he does act like a jackass.''

So she hadn't imagined that Tony was hitting on her. "At least he didn't toss me out on my ear."

He didn't answer and she thought he hadn't heard the comment. Which was okay, since she didn't want to discuss it anyway.

"Tony is all right," Carson said. Outlined by the dash lights his profile was thoughtful. "He's not from around here."

She would have bet good money that Tony knew who she was and what her father had done. "Oh."

"He moved in about six, seven months ago. He takes a lot of business trips."

"What does he do?"

"Computers, communications, something electronic. Whatever he does, it pays well. He has more expensive toys than anyone I know. You don't have to worry about him hassling you or trying to run you off." He steered around a circular driveway and parked in front of a large, two-story house.

She was so tired she had to force her feet to move up the steps onto the wide porch. She searched for flames on her property. Emergency lights pierced the night, but no orange fire glow. She caught a whiff of smoke, but wasn't sure if she smelled the fire or her own hair.

Carson urged her inside and up a set of stairs. Numb, wanting only a place to rest, she stopped where he told her to stop. He turned on a light in a large bathroom with a claw-footed tub.

"Plenty of soap and clean towels in that cabinet. I'll fetch something you can wear."

She wanted to ask why he did this for her, but she was too tired. Across the hall, he turned on a light in another room. "Sleep in here. I'll get the bed made up."

He didn't look at her while he talked. She sensed nervousness or discomfort or maybe he was kicking himself for bringing her here. He should have put her up in jail for the night. Or have her sleep on the porch. Anything had to be better than Frank Shay's daughter sleeping under his roof.

Chapter Four

Clouds ringed the horizon, but Madeline didn't sense an impending storm. A good thing, considering she'd be sleeping outside from now on. She wore men's sweatpants, a T-shirt and a warm-up jacket so big the shoulder seams hung almost to her elbows. Time to see in the daylight the damage done. Carson offered breakfast, but she was too heartbroken over her ruined beadwork to eat.

She lifted her chin and straightened her shoulders. Even in borrowed clothing she had her pride. She approached the police cruiser. Through the open passenger window, she asked, "Shall I ride in back, Chief Cody?"

"Get in the front." He looked as grim and angry as he had last night. With a tan uniform shirt tailored over his muscular chest and arms, his mouth set in a thin line, and dark glasses concealing his eyes, he looked like the kind of cop who'd ticket a nun for jaywalking. She buckled the seat belt and sat rigidly facing forward.

He drove away from the house. "Did you sleep okay?"

That seemed an odd question from an angry man. "I suppose. All things considered."

"Your house is totaled. Are you prepared to face it?"

"I don't have a choice."

"You cannot imagine how sorry I am, Madeline."

His apology stunned her. It almost made her think he wasn't mad at her.

"I knew something like this would happen. I am very sorry."

It was difficult keeping her defenses up when he said things like that. "I don't know what you could have done. I wouldn't have left even if you told me to. I just don't know why you told everybody I was here in the first place." She tried to catch his eye. "I kind of thought we had an agreement."

His mouth tightened. He didn't say another word until a female voice came over the radio. He picked up the mike. "Come again, Wanda? Did you say ten-fifty-four?"

"Dooley Duran just called it in," Wanda replied. "He's at the Shay ranch. You're responding?"

"Ten-four. Notify Morales. Out."

He shot Madeline a puzzled look. "You were alone last night, right?"

She touched her bruised mouth. "Until…you know. What's going on?"

"The fire chief says he has a body."

"At my house?" It occurred to her that whoever set the fire got caught in the flames. "Oh God."

She smelled smoke long before she saw what remained of the house. She covered her nose against the stench. A yellow fire truck and a white SUV with a volunteer fire department logo emblazoned on the door were parked in the yard. The house had been reduced to smoldering embers with only the stone chimney intact. A few framing timbers poked from the ruins like charcoal fingers. Her van was a blackened hulk. The back doors lay twisted several feet away. The tires were black puddles.

It amazed her that she and Carson had escaped serious injury.

Several men garbed in canvas firefighting garb leaned on shovels and watched the smoking fire pit.

When Carson had parked, Madeline stepped out of the cruiser. The acrid air was uncomfortable on her raw throat. Heat waves shimmered over the ruins.

Some of the surrounding foliage was singed. The garage was still standing. Paint had blistered on the wall closest to the house, but otherwise it looked all right. Her beads, tools and finished pieces were in the garage. Heaviness lifted from her shoulders.

Carson stalked toward the men like a boxer revving up for the ring. As much as she longed to see for herself that her work was all right, distracting or annoying Carson right now seemed like a very bad idea.

The oldest of the men pointed at the center of the ruins. Carson leaned over, then straightened and shook his head. He looked at Madeline then at the fire pit then back to her. Curiosity overrode her trepidation. She approached him.

"Are you sure there was no one else with you last night?" Carson asked. He pointed into the center of the ashes where embers glowed. A black bone thrust skyward.

Madeline followed the line of bone until she picked out the blackened dome of a skull. That nasty smell from beneath the house suddenly made sense. Nausea rose and she clapped a hand over her mouth.

"We spotted it," the oldest firefighter said, "and quit digging around. I swear it looks human."

"I swear you're right," Carson said. "Keep working

the perimeter. Stay as far away from the bones as you can, but we don't need a wildfire on top of everything else." He urged Madeline to follow him to the garage.

Madeline couldn't tear her gaze away from the bone reaching skyward.

"Madeline?"

She swallowed hard and winced at the flare-up of pain. "That can't be a person. I absolutely, positively cannot bear to think I was sleeping atop a corpse. Couldn't it be a dog or a coyote? Or even a bear?"

"Wait here." He wanted her in front of the garage door. "I'll be right back."

The longer she stood, the more the reality of the situation came home. Her money had been stashed in the van along with ID, tax records, and application forms for art shows. Her clothes, sleeping bag, camp stove, books, clippings, and all the odds and ends of life were gone.

She peered inside the garage. The burned paint and metal gave off a pungent, chemical odor. Parts of the tin roof had buckled from the heat. Other than smoke hovering around the ceiling, the interior was untouched. The boxes of beads, findings, and tools were as she left them. The finished pieces, wrapped in tissue to keep away dust, sat unharmed on the shelves. The ache in her chest eased.

She touched her throat then slid her finger down to the locket she wore on a ball chain around her neck. It figured it would escape the fire. Her gaze lit on the small box labeled Dumb Stuff. Laughter rose, choking and tight, so she clamped her jaw and covered her mouth, knowing if she started laughing at the absurdity of it all she might never stop.

"Madeline," Carson said. "Do you remember anything else about last night?"

She welcomed the pain of swallowing hard—it killed the urge to laugh. "Only what I told you."

"When I left my house it wasn't much past eight o'clock. Do you always go to sleep that early?"

She searched his face for clues. "What are you getting at?"

"I'm trying to figure out what is going on here."

"Yes, I go to sleep that early. I don't have a television or radio. I don't want to waste fuel, so I don't read at night, either. When the sun goes down, I go to sleep."

"May I see your hands?"

Instinctively she put her hands behind her back. It was ridiculous—she had nothing to hide. She thrust out her hands and he took them into his. His hands were large and suntanned. They made hers look small as a child's. He studied her scraped, swollen knuckles.

"You did this when you escaped out a window?"

She jerked her hands from his grasp. "You think I killed a man then set my house on fire to cover it up?"

"I'm thinking you were assaulted. I want to know if you fought back."

"I told you already. I put boards over the windows because the glass was broken." She waggled her hands at him. "I busted boards with my hands."

He peered inside the garage. "Looks like you saved your belongings."

She bristled and steel studded her spine. How *dare* he? "Like father, like daughter? I must be a killer because I'm a Shay?"

"I need to know what happened."

"Oh yeah, I saved my belongings all right. Except

for the van, which is my only transportation. And my clothes and my cash and all my camping gear and food and dishes. Oh, and can't forget, my toothbrush!'' She pointed into the garage. "*That* is my work. It didn't burn because even I have to get lucky sometimes.'' She pointed at the van. "*That* was my life. But who cares, my life sucks rocks anyway.'' Clamping her arms over her chest, she turned her back on him.

She was not going to cry. She refused. She'd set herself on fire before giving him the satisfaction of reducing her to tears.

Seconds ticked by. Her skin prickled in apprehension. If he arrested her, she would sit in jail because there wasn't a person living who'd bail her out.

"This is my job,'' Carson said. "I have to ask the hard questions. You're the victim, not a suspect. I'm sorry if I implied otherwise.''

She was such a softie when it came to big men with gentle voices. "I don't know if it means anything, but every once in a while a really awful smell would fill up the house. I thought an animal had died under there.''

"You never investigated?''

"I don't care for snakes and spiders. So no.''

His broad chest rose and fell as if with a sigh. "What is that in the garage?''

"My beadwork. I'm supposed to display it at a juried show in Santa Fe. I have twelve more pieces to finish.'' She couldn't help a wry laugh at the irony. She had left Whiteriver because her mother made life unbearable. Some safe haven this turned out to be.

"The sheriff is on his way and so is the medical examiner. I'll have to wait for their findings before I let you go back to Whiteriver.''

"Back to Whiteriver? What are you talking about?''

"Isn't that where you live? Where your mother lives?"

She slumped against the garage wall and covered her eyes with a hand. She didn't think the police chief was being deliberately thick. He didn't understand. "This is my home."

"What about your mother's house?"

She clamped her mouth shut. Old habits died hard, especially the habit of keeping family nastiness to herself.

He folded his arms, waiting for an answer.

"My mother is not…right. She's an alcoholic and bipolar. When she's depressed she wants to kill herself. When she's manic she wants to kill me. Then my father left me this stupid ranch." The end of her rope looked very near. "It's impossible for me to go back."

He turned his attention to men shoveling dirt onto the ashes. When he faced her again, his expression had eased. "Is there anyone you can call? Someone who can help?"

She wasn't the type to ask for help. She wished she were. "Maybe."

"You can't stay here."

"If the well isn't fouled, I can."

"It's a crime scene. And there's the small matter of figuring out who set the fire."

Good point, she thought reluctantly. "I can't go anywhere without my beads. They're all I have left."

"I have a padlock in the cruiser to lock up the garage. Your beads will be safe until we can get back here with my truck so you can load everything up. We'll figure out a place for you to stay."

She didn't trust him. She couldn't trust him. Even if he acted out of a sense of duty or even altruism, sooner or later he would remember who she was and what she represented.

She eyed her dirty bare feet. She didn't even have a pair of shoes or change of underwear. Her Apache ancestors had trekked through the desert and mountains barefoot and half-naked, relying on their wits for food, water and shelter. She wasn't that tough.

"Okay," she said.

Madeline waited in the cruiser. Carson padlocked the garage and placed a seal on the door, whether to protect her belongings or insure uncontaminated evidence she wasn't certain. When Sergeant Morales arrived, he and Carson stretched yellow police tape around the yard. They walked the area, stopping every once in a while to plant yellow flags.

She longed for something to drink. Her throat felt lined with metal shavings and it still hurt to swallow. Watching Carson offered diversion, but it was a dangerous pastime in that the more she watched, the more attractive he looked.

He acted as if saving her life was no big deal, that anyone would have done it. The twisted remains of the van told her better. He had risked his life. She rubbed her throat, trying to push away the discomfort and rub away the yearning to hear his gentle voice again.

She tore her gaze away. Looking at the house, knowing it held a body, made her skin crawl.

A red Jeep Wrangler, outfitted with big tires, big lights, reinforced roll bars and a winch roared into the yard. Tony Rule hopped out, swinging a white paper bag.

Carson waved him back. "You can't be here, Tony. It's a crime scene."

Tony held out the bag. "Doughnuts. A bribe to let

me inspect the damage." He whistled. "Damn. Hard to believe this whole area didn't go up in flames. Is that a van? I'd have paid to watch that blow up."

Carson pulled at his jaw and lowered his face. Madeline believed he was trying not to laugh at Tony's irreverence. "You have to go. Now."

"Come on. I love living here, but you gotta admit it's boring as hell. This is the most interesting thing that's happened since I moved in." He jerked a thumb toward the cruiser. "Watching the cops in action, up close and personal, is the chance of a lifetime. I'll stay over there. Quiet as a mouse." He made a zippering motion across his mouth.

"No can do," Carson said. "Beat it."

Tony loosed an exaggerated sigh. "Can't blame a guy for trying." He tossed the bag at Carson, who caught it with quick gracefulness that was magical to watch. "Keep the doughnuts anyway. I hear you coppers can't live without them."

Instead of returning to the Jeep, he sauntered over to the cruiser.

Carson harrumphed.

"Just a sec," Tony said. He leaned an arm on the cruiser's roof so he loomed over Madeline.

She knew his type. He had that cocky, loose-hipped air that said *I'm sexy and you know it, so why fight it?* "How are you doing this morning, Miss Shay?"

"Fine."

"I notice your house is in need of a few repairs. You are more than welcome to camp out at my place."

Incredulous over his flirtatious tone, she wished he would take her silence as a hint and leave.

Carson headed their way. He was furious. Warned by

her alarm, Tony shoved away from the cruiser and held up his hands.

"I'm leaving, I'm leaving."

"I don't play around at crime scenes," Carson said. "Especially when a death is involved."

"Who died?"

"Don't know yet and it's none of your business."

Head down, his manner conciliatory, Tony returned to his Jeep. He started the engine then yelled, "I'll bring the beer later! You can give me the juicy details then." He wheeled the Jeep in a tight circle and drove away.

Carson handed the bag of doughnuts to Madeline. He pulled off his hat and used a white handkerchief to wipe sweat from his brow and neck. "Walking, talking attitude," he said with a chuckle. "Pete will handle things until the sheriff and coroner get here. I could use some coffee to go with those doughnuts."

Carson slid behind the steering wheel and started the engine. Halfway to the road, a blue car blocked the driveway. "Damn it!" Carson muttered. "Did somebody put up a sign when I wasn't looking?"

Madeline sank lower on the seat. "Is that a reporter?"

"Worse." He put the transmission in Park and shoved open the door. "Mr. Bannerman," he yelled. "Back up the car and go back to town."

The insurance man popped into view. "What happened? I heard there was a fire. What's going on?"

"Hope what he's looking for wasn't in the house," Madeline said.

"Please, Chief Cody, I need access."

"If you don't vacate these premises I will arrest you for obstruction."

Bannerman wrung his hands and looked about wildly

as if aid might suddenly appear. Carson stepped around the open door. Bannerman dived into the car and slammed the door. The tires sprayed the cruiser with gravel and dust swallowed the blue sedan.

Carson picked up the radio mike. When the dispatcher answered, he told her to contact the sheriff and request a deputy to stand guard on Hoshonee Road. Rubberneckers and reporters would be out in force.

Madeline wiped away a smirk. "You're one mean cop."

"Yes, ma'am." A slow smile captured his mouth and lit up his face.

Madeline glimpsed the real Carson Cody behind the mask of sorrow. A thump in her belly warned her that romantic notions were inappropriate, not to mention ludicrous. Still, she imagined the man he used to be before her father had destroyed his life.

"We need to talk," he said. "I have some hard questions. Are you up for it?"

"As long as I'm not a suspect."

"Tell me about the smell in the house."

How did one describe a smell? "It gagged me. I didn't smell it all the time. Sometimes it was unbearable."

"You smelled it when you first arrived? When exactly was that?"

"March fifteenth. I was up at a bead show in Minnesota. I hoped the house would be livable, but it would have taken me months to shovel out the trash. So I set up camp in the kitchen and closed off the rest. Truth is, I thought the smell came from something the vandals had left behind. Dead skunks or a deer. I never imagined it was a person." Gooseflesh rose and she scrubbed her arms. "My head doesn't believe in ghosts, but my heart sure does."

"Minnesota, huh? That's a long way to go to buy some beads."

"I don't go just to buy. I go to sell. That's why I'm here, to get ready for a show in Santa Fe. I'm going for broke with my big art pieces. I hope to catch the eye of major collectors and gallery owners."

"Ah." He nodded understanding.

"I travel a lot. I'm used to living out of my van." She sighed. "I'm going to miss her. We traveled a lot of miles together."

"No insurance?"

"Liability." She sighed again. "No insurance on the house, either. One good thing is I already paid for a booth in Santa Fe. Now I just have to figure out how to get there."

He turned onto the drive leading up the mesa. "Talk to me about your father. He wrote you from prison, right? Did he talk about his crimes?"

"You mean, the last time he was locked up?"

"Yes."

She fiddled with the jacket zipper. "I didn't read them."

"Why?"

"Because they're all the same, okay? A lot of whining and promises he can't keep."

"Did he contact you before his last conviction? Give you money?"

Goose bumps made her shiver. "Money?"

He glanced between her and the narrow road. He slowed to let a pair of quails race to safety. "He did, didn't he?"

She shifted uncomfortably and fiddled with the seat-belt strap. She grew very aware of his uniform and badge and riding in an official police cruiser. "Suppose he did, but I didn't keep it—will I get in trouble?"

"What did he give you?"

She rubbed the locket through the T-shirt. Created from a soda can, it was clunky but charming. As much as she hated her father, she could not throw away his art. "Ten thousand dollars cash."

Carson's mouth dropped open.

"He said he won the lottery."

"When exactly did he give it to you?"

"I don't know exactly. Right before he went to prison, I guess." She wondered if she had unwittingly aided her father's criminal career. "I should have turned it over to the police. I didn't want to get involved." She studied his reaction. "I didn't keep it. I donated it to the Indian school."

"The whole ten thousand dollars?"

"Every bit of it. Ill-gotten goods are bad luck." She chewed on a thumbnail. "Am I in trouble?"

"Did he give it to you personally? Drop it on your doorstep? What?"

"A box of money through the mail. I remember looking for a return address, but there wasn't one. I think it was postmarked in Phoenix. Am I in trouble?"

"Not with me. What about after his release? Did he visit you?"

Not in trouble with him—that left a lot of other law agencies to screw up her life. "I was in Tucson in February, then Chicago, Detroit and Milwaukee. I didn't return to Arizona until about a week…before it happened. He did visit Mama though." She rolled her eyes at the memory. "He divorced her."

"I thought they were married when he died."

"And I thought they divorced years ago. In thirty years, I bet they never spent more than two or three years together. He told Mama the story about winning the lottery and she was never getting a cent. That's why she's mad at me. He had a jailhouse last will and testament." She paused. "If he and Mama were married, she would inherit half his estate. She hired a lawyer to check out the lottery story. I knew it was a lie, and the lawyer proved it, but Mama is convinced he used a fake name to collect his winnings."

Wishing for something to kick, she slumped on the seat. Half the people on the reservation were convinced she possessed a ton of money, which made her a stuck-up snot who refused to share.

Carson made a musing sound.

"Is the money he gave me connected to the body under the house? To the other…things he did?"

He picked up the radio mike. "Ten-four, dispatch. This is Cody."

"Chief," a woman said over the radio, "that insurance salesman is back. He's bouncing around the station, pestering everybody for information. Can I give him your twenty?"

He waited a moment before depressing the button. "That's a negative, dispatch. Tell him to leave a number where I can reach him later today."

"What is your twenty?"

"I'm ten-ten for the next hour. Out." He slipped the mike back onto its holder.

Madeline cocked her head. "I didn't understand any of that."

"Ten-twenty means my location. Ten-ten means I'm at home."

They reached the house. She studied the turn-of-the-century styling with tall windows, a peaked roof and wraparound porch. The house was big enough for several families. She followed him onto the porch. Maybe it was the dusty flowerpots holding only dirt or maybe the utter silence, but the place had a sad, deserted air.

The house was clean, but the deserted atmosphere was strong. Last night she had imagined ghosts. The kitchen wasn't too bad, with brightly colored tiles forming a backsplash and cheery curtains on the window over the sink. Carson looked her up and down. His gaze was impassive, almost clinical, as if he studied a piece of wood.

"What size shoe do you wear?"

"An eight."

"I can't believe I forgot shoes." His tone was faintly admonishing, as if faulting her for not asking. "You and Jill are about the same size. Have a seat. I'll be back."

Madeline held a ladder-back chair and looked around at the painted cupboards, the old-fashioned linoleum on the floor and the massive knotty-pine table that could easily seat twelve. Jill Cody had cooked here, laughed here, and eaten meals with her husband and friends. Madeline felt so sad the back of her eyes hurt.

Carson's return startled her. He was a big man, but his step was silent as a cat's. He carried a stack of clothing. A pair of sandals dangled from his hand.

"This will fit better." He handed her the clothing. The sandals had tire-rubber soles and adjustable straps. Madeline owned—used to own—a pair just like them.

"You don't have to do this, Chief Cody."

"Call me Carson."

"You don't have to do this, Carson."

He shifted his weight from foot to foot, and rubbed

the back of his neck. "Yes, ma'am, I do need to do this. Now I'm going on back to your house. Help yourself to the kitchen."

"What about my beads?"

"It might be tomorrow before I can fetch them. You have my word, they'll be safe."

"You won't confiscate them for evidence or anything?"

He smiled. It was sudden and blinding and genuine. Years dropped from his face and good humor eased the lines etched into his forehead. His smile transfixed her, humbled her. It was a rare gift indeed.

"I don't recollect ever hearing about beads being a cause of death."

He actually teased her. She lowered her gaze to the bundle of clothing. He truly was decent. Most surprising of all, she considered him trustworthy. Which was strange, because she rarely trusted anybody. She silently accepted the apology he made earlier.

He pulled a pad of paper from a drawer and wrote on it. "You know how to call nine-one-one. Here's my cell number if you need anything else." He drew a deep breath, expanding his chest. "I don't want to scare you, but you have to consider the possibility it was more than arson. It could be attempted murder."

She nodded solemnly,.

"I'll see about getting a deputy to prevent anyone from driving up here. Whether I can or not, I don't want you opening the doors. I don't care if it's your best friend from second grade, do not open the door."

She touched her brow in salute. "Yes, sir."

"Do you know the name of the attorney who checked out your father's lottery story?"

"No. He couldn't have been that good since Mama

rarely has money. Doesn't pay her bills when she does.'' She stepped back to better see his face. "He didn't actually win the lottery, did he? Can a person collect winnings with a fake name?"

"I don't know what he was up to. That's what I'm trying to figure out. Lock up behind me."

She walked him to the door. "Thank you, Carson."

"Don't mention it, ma'am." He settled his hat on his head and left.

Chapter Five

Carson returned to the crime scene. A funny feeling gnawed at him. A tightness across his diaphragm, a low ache deep in his belly and worry in his heart.

He had felt this way ever since he pulled a pair of jeans from a drawer, a shirt from the closet and picked up a pair of shoes. Jill's clothing for the daughter of her murderer. He decided it must be guilt. The ache spread through his abdomen. He'd resisted every suggestion about clearing out Jill's belongings. After he moved out of the big bedroom they once shared, he hadn't opened the door. Until today.

He'd given Jill's things to Madeline. Right, wrong?

It couldn't be wrong. Jill was the first to leap into action when a neighbor hit hard times. He had come home several times to a stripped pantry because of food drives. She'd been active at church, volunteered on civic committees and for the health clinic, and put in untold hours as an advisor for the 4-H club. If she were alive, she'd outfit Madeline head to toe, set her up in the best bedroom in the house and never think twice about it.

A deputy guarded the entrance to the driveway. He stepped aside for Carson's cruiser.

Carson didn't recognize the young man. "Any problems?"

"I turned away some locals and a reporter. Nobody gave me any trouble."

The fire trucks were gone, though the fire chief remained on the scene. Carson glowered at Dooley Duran. The old house had gone up so quick it was doubtful the Ruff fire department could have saved anything even with an immediate response. Even so, Dooley let his personal bias get in the way of his job and Carson considered that a grave sin.

A gray haze hung over the wide clearing. There were two sheriff's vehicles and the medical examiner's van outside the perimeter of police tape. Pete Morales waved at him. Several men picked through the ashes. They wore tall, rubber boots and caps with bright yellow letters proclaiming Sheriff.

Pete sauntered over to the cruiser. "This is weird, chief. You might want to hear what the M.E. has to say."

"As long as he doesn't tell me it's one of the Harrigans."

"You thought that, too, huh? Want me to find out where Matt and Sug were last night?" Pete asked.

"We're turning this investigation over to the sheriff. I don't want a whisper of conflict of interest to screw up a conviction."

Carson watched from the sidelines while the forensics specialists used plaster of Paris to lift tire prints and others picked through debris. The medical examiner pulled blackened bones from the ashes and laid them out on plastic sheeting. The skull was unmistakably human.

"Looks like my wife's cooking," Dooley said.

"Nice," Carson said. "First you let him burn, then you make jokes."

Dooley's face turned crimson and he slunk away.

"John," Carson said to the sheriff's lead investigator. "What do you think?"

The investigator pulled off his cap and armed sweat off his face. "No doubt about it. Some sort of accelerant. My guess is kerosene. I'll let you know for sure once the samples have gone through the lab."

Carson nodded. Madeline had no electricity out here. He'd ask her if she used a kerosene lamp. "The body?"

"That's the funny part. Not enough meat on the bones to put up his dukes." He referred to the way many burned bodies were found with the arms drawn into a boxer's pose. "It's been under there quite a while."

Relief rippled through him. If Madeline had killed one of her attackers, it would have been in self-defense, but that wouldn't do her any good in Ruff.

"Man or woman?"

John shrugged. "The M.E. isn't saying. A lot of the bones crumbled like dust. It'll be tough making an ID. The woman who lives here, does she have a story?"

"She said she smelled something bad. Guess the body was stashed in the crawl space. Did you find anything pointing to a suspect?"

"I picked up some pieces of glass and a metal fuel can. It's possible I can lift some prints. I'll need prints from the home owner so I can eliminate her."

"It's Madeline Shay, John. Frank Shay's daughter."

John took a step to the side and lifted his face. "So it's true? Woman's either sheep-stupid or got clackers like a brass bull. Where is she now?"

"Protective custody."

John pointed at the garage. "What's with the lock and seal?"

"She's an artist. I promised to protect her belongings. I'll unlock it for you."

While he sorted through keys, his cell phone rang. Caller ID read Pay Phone. He answered with a curt, "Cody."

"Chief Cody, this is Ivan Bannerman. I need to talk to you right now."

His bordering-on-hysterical tone rasped Carson's raw nerves. "It'll have to wait."

"Did you find the money?"

Carson indicated John should wait. He walked away a few feet and lowered his voice. "The money is at the bottom of my priority list right now, Mr. Bannerman. If anyone stumbles over it, I'll let you know. Until then, don't tie up my phone."

"You have to let me know first! Mutual Security and Assurance has policies. Procedures. If it ends up in a police evidence room, I'll lose my job."

And this was Carson's problem? "I'll keep you posted."

"Miss Shay has to let me search now."

"Nobody is searching anything until the investigation is complete. Goodbye, sir." He depressed the off button. He considered turning off the unit altogether, but Madeline might need him. He tucked the phone into its holster.

He unlocked the garage for John. "I promised the owner not to disturb her work."

"In and out like a burglar." John checked the settings on his camera and entered the garage.

Carson sought out Pete. "Do me a favor. Call the tribal police on Fort Apache. See if they can find out if a sizable cash donation was made to the Indian school. It would have been around four years ago, in January or February.''

Pete's face wrinkled in puzzlement. ''What's this all about?''

''Just do it. Be sure and ask them what the exact amount was and who donated it. I'll fill you in later.'' He nodded toward the trees. ''Here's the sheriff. Have you got a copy of Madeline's statement?''

Sheriff Gerald Poulton arrived. Carson and the investigator brought him up to speed. Pete turned over a transcript of Madeline's statement, gave Carson a considering look then went to his vehicle to use the mobile phone.

Carson drew Gerald to the edge of the yard, far from curious ears. Gerald Poulton had a leathery complexion and sharp blue eyes. His uniform consisted of a gold badge pinned to the pocket of a white dress shirt open at the throat, black denim trousers and a pistol in a tooled leather holster that matched his boots. He had a crafty look that came with age and experience. As a boy, Carson had wanted to grow up to be a lawman just like Sheriff Gerald.

''Remember the Worldwide Parcel hijacking?''

''Everybody remembers. Why?''

''I think Frank Shay was involved.''

Gerald cocked back his white straw cowboy hat. ''Where did you come up with that?''

Carson heard what Gerald left unspoken: *Where did you come up with a crazy-fool idea like that?*

''An insurance investigator from Nevada is convinced Shay got away with the money. He thinks thirty million dollars is buried right here.'' He pointed to the dirt at their feet.

"Like to know what that insurance fella is sniffing." Gerald shook his head and grinned. "Trust me, Frank Shay rates right up there in the top ten dumbest criminals I ever ran across. There wasn't much he ever got away with."

"I think it's possible."

Gerald dropped a callused hand on Carson's shoulder. "Want my advice? Stay the hell away from anything to do with Frank Shay. You don't need the aggravation."

"I'm running down names. Checking out details. It might explain why he did what he did."

"Or you can run around chasing wild hares and get your heart broke all over again. Drop it, boy. Trust me on this. You can't do your job if you're chasing ghosts." Gerald indicated the M.E.'s van where two men loaded the remains. "Any ideas about Mr. Bones?"

Carson swallowed his rising temper. Maybe Gerald was right. Maybe it was his own thirst for answers that made him believe Bannerman.

If only he could forget the delivery van and ten thousand dollars given to Frank's daughter.

"It isn't one of the Harrigan boys, but I suspect they were here last night. They weren't happy about Shay's daughter."

"And you? Has to be hard laying eyes on that woman."

It was, but it wasn't. Carson wasn't magnanimous enough to forgive and forget what Frank Shay had done. Truth be told, if Madeline had resembled her father he might have a harder time being around her.

"I'm fine," he said.

Gerald nodded, but there was a skeptical twist to his

lips. "And that's why you keep telling Ruthie you're too busy to come to Sunday dinner? You go to work. You sit at home in that big, old empty house. Funny way of being fine."

Carson bristled. "This isn't about me."

Gerald's eyes disappeared into sun-dried wrinkles. "You and me haven't had a sit-down and a beer since it happened. You shut me out. Far as I know, you shut everybody out. I know you're hurting, Carson. Damned if I don't know how bad. But some pain needs sharing. I'm your friend. You need to remember that."

An ache filled his chest and his throat grew thick. "I don't need friends right now. I need good cops to solve this crime."

"I'm sixty-nine years old, boy. I've buried relatives, friends and two stillborn babies. Do you honestly think I don't know what you're going through?"

"You have all you need from me." He walked away.

Maybe Gerald knew about grief and sorrow, but he didn't know Carson's pain. Nobody did. Nobody ever would.

At the garage the investigator was replacing the padlock. He slapped a fresh seal on the door.

"Find anything?" Carson asked.

"A bunch of beads, small tools, and some personal gewgaws. No accelerant. Not even a match."

"Can we dig up the floor? See if our victim has some friends?"

"Before we go doing that, we need to figure out how old the concrete pad is and if it's compatible with the time of death. I can bring a cadaver dog through. A dog might tell us if there's a body." John winked. "Sheriff gets testy when I start rattling bulldozer keys without probable cause."

Carson knew men with access to earthmovers and bulldozers. He ought to dig up the entire ranch. Like Madeline said, ill-gotten gains were bad luck. Returning the money to its rightful owners might halt the mounting body count.

MADELINE STARTLED from sleep. A dark shape loomed over her. She jerked upright off the sofa and gasped. Her mind and body froze up.

The shape stepped back. ''Sorry, didn't mean to scare you,'' Carson said.

She pressed a hand over her pounding heart. Gloom said the sun went down. Her eyes adjusted quickly. She watched him settle his cowboy hat on a peg and unbuckle his utility belt. Feeling guilty about being caught snoozing on his sofa, she stood and folded her hands over her belly.

''Sorry I'm so late,'' he said. ''The mayor caught me at the police station. I got enough earfuls to last a year or two.'' He turned on a lamp.

His hair looked black, his skin dark. The proud jut of his cheekbones and nose made her wonder if he had Indian blood in him.

''How are you feeling?''

Lots of cool water and a nap had left her feeling a hundred-percent better. She touched her tongue to the scab on her lip. The swelling had gone down. ''I'm fine.'' His perusal made her self-conscious about wearing his dead wife's clothing.

''The body has nothing to do with the fire. M.E. says the bones were under the house at least six months, maybe longer.''

She shuddered. She wouldn't even pass a graveyard

at night, and she'd been sleeping atop a corpse? "Do you know who it is?"

"Won't even know if it's a man or a woman until the M.E. figures it out." He walked down the hallway to the kitchen. Madeline followed. "Do you remember anything else about the fire?"

"No."

He hung the utility belt on a hook inside the pantry. He moved around without looking at her. "This is a big old house and I'm hardly ever here." He unbuttoned his uniform shirt and opened the freezer compartment in the refrigerator. "Don't think I'm casting crumbs. I'm not." He pulled a foil-covered dish from the freezer. "You can stay here until we get your situation straightened out." He turned on the oven. "It's no bother to me and no one will bother you. Nobody has to know you're here. You'll be safe."

It took a moment before she got her wits about her to speak. "I can't let you do that, Carson."

He was walking up the stairs.

The trait she disliked most in herself was her instinctive distrust of kindness. When people were cruel, she knew where they were coming from. Kindness was too often a thin mask over darker motives. She couldn't for the life of her imagine why Carson Cody was being so nice.

When he returned, he wore a ragged T-shirt with A.S.U. emblazoned on the front and a pair of faded blue jeans. He still wouldn't look at her. He slid the casserole into the oven. "Have to take care of my horse."

"Carson."

He stopped, shoulders hunched.

"Thank you for the offer, but I can't accept. You've done too much for me already."

He opened the door. "You don't have much choice." Before she could reply, he slipped out of the house.

She slumped against a counter. Carson Cody was one of the strangest men she'd ever met. She could not accept the offer, but she forced herself to appreciate the kindness behind it.

"OH, THANK YOU, thank you." Breathlessly Madeline peeled tissue paper from the beaded vessel she called *Wildfire*. Sixteen inches tall and shaped like a gourd with a curved swanlike neck and fat bottom, it was a piece she loved so much she hated putting it up for sale. Subtle shades of red, orange and yellow swirled against a background of electric blue and soot-black. Wings and ruffles of beads formed flickering flames.

She beamed at Carson. Everything was here, even the empty paint can she used for disposing of bits of thread and broken beads. The cardboard boxes smelled of smoke, but nothing was damaged.

She had spent a second night on the narrow bed squeezed into a bedroom used for storage and hadn't slept well despite clean sheets and a firm mattress. Ghostly whispers seemed to emanate from the walls. No matter how she tossed and turned, she couldn't stop thinking about Carson sleeping only a few feet away. So this was it. She couldn't impose any longer. She couldn't shove ugly reminders into his face.

Good intentions be damned, now she had her beads. She itched to get to work, to make up some lost time. Part of her said she ought to be ashamed of her selfishness, but it was weak in the face of her yearning. Mama had alcohol, Madeline had art. Both were slaves to obsession.

"That's…" His voice trailed as if the words were in

there but he couldn't grab them. "I've never seen anything like that. It's beautiful."

She set the vessel on the table where light sparkled and shimmered against the cut beads, giving the piece a life of its own. His compliment filled her with warmth. "I'm hoping folks at the Santa Fe show think the same thing."

He reached for the piece but stopped before touching it. "How do you do that? Glue?"

"They're sewn on one bead at a time. I never use glue on vessels. You can't know how happy I am this didn't burn up. I'd never be able to replace it."

"I'm sorry you lost everything else."

"I knew the risk when I came here." That was only half a lie. She had convinced herself that no one would know she was in the area. She poked through a box and found the phoenix vessel, with the thread still wrapped neatly around the neck and the needle tucked between the beads.

"I have to go back to town. The kitchen table is yours, so you can work. Same rule as yesterday. Do not, under any circumstances, open the door."

Wanting to accept burned like hunger. She had no money for rent, no valuables to pawn, no way of even promising payment. Then she remembered the casserole he had fed her last night. A gray mush with overcooked noodles and colorless vegetables tasting of canned soup and salt. He kept a tidy house, but he didn't know a lick about putting together a decent meal. "I can cook."

He brightened with interest. "Yeah?"

"I've been told my biscuits are worth sitting down to and I respect a good cut of beef." She lifted a shoulder. "I can earn my keep. For a few days, until I can figure out what to do."

His focus went distant. He looked relaxed and not so weighted down this morning. His eyes were almost pretty, being so light against his dark complexion. In them were signs of hungering for good food.

"It might be more than a few days," he said. "There's the investigation and the fact that someone tried to seriously hurt you."

She opened her mouth to protest, but he spoke first. "Can you make a pot roast? You know, with onions and carrots and dark gravy?"

"I can."

His smile entranced her. Her naturally lusty nature, kept so carefully hidden, bubbled to the surface. She drank in the craggy, handsome lines of his face and the powerful musculature of his neck. She dared let her attention slip to the breadth of his shoulders and his lean belly snugged beneath the heavily laden utility belt. Imagining what lay beneath the tailored shirt and trousers warmed her blood. She had a weakness for big men with brawny arms and sexy voices and slow smiles. Carson had the slowest smile she had ever witnessed.

"Okay then," he said. "There should be a roast in the freezer and produce on the bottom shelves in the pantry. Feel free to rummage for anything else you might need. I'll be back around six-thirty."

She rested her chin on her fist and frowned. Of all the places to find herself, this would have been the last she'd have ever imagined.

As engine noise faded, absorbed by the sough of wind against the house and the rumble of the swamp cooler, inspiration captured her. Within minutes she had her work in progress set up on the table and fresh wax on the thread. She picked up a bead and settled in to work.

Midmorning, unable to ignore the crick in her neck any longer, she set down the needle. She rose and stretched and rolled her head from side to side. She poured a cup of coffee. It was bitter and burned, having sat on the coffeemaker for hours, but she needed the caffeine jolt. Down the hall, through the front room, she stood at the window and studied the day. Thunderheads towered over the far horizon, brilliant white and steel-gray.

A movement flashed across her peripheral vision. She ducked and coffee splashed her shirt. She set the cup on the floor then crept to a window and peered outside.

Tony Rule jogged around the circular driveway. He wore very short running shorts and no shirt. A white sweatband was stark against his black hair. His skin gleamed in the sunshine.

Madeline was impressed that he'd been able to run up the mesa from his cabin. He ran a second circuit around the driveway. She wondered if he knew she watched him. He had come by the house last night. Madeline considered it prudent to stay upstairs while the men drank a beer on the porch.

Don't open the door even for her best friend from second grade, Carson had said. She didn't like following orders, but her throat was still sore from smoke inhalation and the cuts on her hands were tender. Good enough reasons to accept his caution.

Tony slowed to a walk and shook his arms and hands. He walked around the house. Curious, Madeline crept from window to window, trying to follow his progress.

His face popped into view. She tried to scream, but all that emerged was a strangled croak. She clutched the shirt material over her heart.

''Madeline!'' He didn't have an ounce of body fat

and every muscle was sharply defined. His model-handsome face was greasy with sweat. "I didn't know you were here."

A nail prevented the window from opening more than a few inches. She touched the nail. Not even her best friend… "What are you doing?"

The wattage of his smile increased. "Stealing water from the faucet. How about some ice?"

"Carson isn't here."

"All the better says the big bad wolf. How are you doing? How are you feeling?"

She'd feel a whole lot better if she knew what to do. Tony's initial surprise meant Carson hadn't told his neighbor about her staying in the house. He was serious about her not opening the door to anyone. "I have work to do. Nice seeing you again." She dropped the curtain and returned to the kitchen.

Water rushed in pipes. The kitchen clock ticked off the seconds. When the water stopped, she relaxed. Far better for Tony to believe she was rude than for Carson to think she was stupid.

She glanced at the paper where Carson had written his cell phone number. No sense bothering him over nothing.

CARSON SLID into the leatherette booth across the table from Judy Green. On the walk to the diner, he had practiced in his head a nice way to fire Judy. There was no nice way. She smiled at him and his ears burned.

The lunch crowd had dispersed from the Big Rim Diner. Carson could tolerate the speculative stares and whispers from the few customers lingering over pie and coffee. Waitresses cleared tables and wiped down booth seats, while complaining loudly about the cheapskates who tied up tables and left miserly tips.

Across the street, old Luke sat on the stone steps, an American flag stuck in the planter beside him, and a handwritten sign saying Only Veterans Deserve To Vote. He held a newspaper and looked for someone to argue with.

The front-page story in today's paper was about the fire on the Shay ranch. Dooley Duran was quoted regarding the suspicious origins of the fire and the valiant efforts that had prevented the fire from spreading. The sheriff gave a short statement about the unidentified body. The story mentioned Madeline's name several times, so anyone who had missed the gossip about her arrival, or didn't believe it, now had the truth in black-and-white.

"So what happened to that woman?" Judy asked. She had arrived before him and picked through a limp salad. "You know, *his* daughter. I hear she killed a guy and set the house on fire to cover it up. I wouldn't be surprised considering her background and all. Apples don't fall far, you know. Does scare me a bit to know she's running around. Or did the sheriff pick her up?"

Her chatter eased his conscience. Around Ruff, the best ways to spread news were the telephone, television and tell Judy. It was time for a change. He hated Judy's cooking and he was tired of everyone knowing the intimate details of his life.

"I asked you to meet me here…I, uh, don't quite know how to say this, Judy. I'll just come out and say it. I don't need your services right now. I have to let you go."

"Come again?"

"It's not like I'm firing you," he said. "I appreciate all you've done for me."

"You can dress it in pretty words all you like," she said, "but I'm still losing my job. You ain't made complaints. What's the matter?"

A waitress set a cup of coffee in front of Carson. He thanked her, but she didn't go far. Carson stirred the coffee until the waitress gave up on eavesdropping. By then Judy went red in the face and her eyes were watery. He'd rather be in the midst of a shoot-out with bank robbers than sitting with a weepy woman.

"Think of this as a vacation."

"A vacation won't pay the electric bill!"

"Beth Robertson is hiring over at the Double View Motel."

"Beth only hires illegals. They work cheap."

Sometimes, Carson thought, given half a chance to escape the small minds and petty prejudices of Ruff, he'd jump at it. "I'm sorry, Judy, I don't need you right now. That's that." He brought out his checkbook. "I'll pay you two weeks' salary because this is such short notice."

Judy slumped and twirled a strand of honey-colored hair around her finger. She was in her midtwenties with a pleasantly pretty face—though not so pretty at the moment with the way she scowled. "I thought you liked me."

"I do like you. This is nothing personal." He filled out a check, tore it from the book and handed it over.

She wrinkled her nose as she read it. "I mean, *like* me. You know, the way I like you. You have to be lonesome in that big house. It's not right for a man to live the way you do. Without a woman and all."

If there was any sexual attraction between them, he'd

missed it. "I have to get back to work." He scooted out of the booth.

"Carson, wait—"

"If I gave you any ideas, I'm sorry."

Her mouth twisted in an ugly grimace. "You men are all alike."

Alarms jangled in his head. He searched his memory for anything he might have done—an affectionate word, a touch—anything at all to make her think he considered her as anything other than an employee. His conscience was clear.

He jammed his hat on his head and made his escape.

Chapter Six

Carson hoped he never had to do that again. Firing police officers was an unpleasant aspect of his job, but sometimes he had no choice. Although a few fired officers had threatened revenge, none ever cried. Judy unsettled him.

Pete snagged him as soon as he entered the station. "You know that question you asked me yesterday? About the Indian school?"

"My office." Carson closed the door. "You found something good?"

"Four years ago, February tenth to be exact, an anonymous donor dumped a shoe box full of cash on the doorstep. Ten thousand bucks."

"I'll be damned." Carson leaned back in his chair. He folded his hands over his stomach, amazed as much by Madeline's selflessness as he was by Bannerman's snitch telling the truth. "You're sure it was anonymous? They weren't playing cagey with you?"

"I talked to Joey Bando, tribal police. I trust him."

"Have a seat. You aren't going to believe this," Carson said.

Wanda opened the door and stuck her head inside. "Lieutenant Imagia is on the phone, Chief."

She could have buzzed the intercom, but Wanda did not consider a closed door a hindrance.

"Thank you."

Wanda sniffed in indignation. "State police best not be sticking their noses into our arson investigation."

"Thank you, Wanda, that will be all. Close the door, please." He picked up the phone.

"I passed Shay's vitals to a friend of mine in Las Vegas," Paul Imagia said. "Witnesses can't ID his mug shot and there aren't any fingerprint matches."

Carson slouched, disappointed. Frank Shay had come up with ten large somewhere, but an anonymous snitch wasn't enough evidence to put him in the middle of a thirty-million-dollar heist.

"However," Paul said, "I did some checking into Shay's arrest down in Phoenix. He was arrested less than a week after the hijacking. According to the arrest report, Shay was buying rounds and throwing around hundred-dollar bills like play money. He took a dislike to a biker type and refused to buy him drinks. That's when the fight broke out. Shay damn near killed the man with a pool cue."

"Was any of the money taken into evidence?"

"Nope. But it gets better. Shay posted his own bond, in cash. One week later he actually shows up for court and, against the advice of his attorney, pleads guilty. Didn't even try for a plea bargain. I talked to the D.A. who handled the case. He says he's never had anyone do that."

Carson doodled a fanciful question mark on the desk blotter. "Let me get this straight. He gets busted for a charge even a half-asleep public defender can plead down to a misdemeanor. Instead he bonds out, actually shows up and risks having the judge come down hard on him for being a habitual offender?''

"Crazy, isn't it?''

"Yeah.''

"I know you, Carson,'' Paul said. "You don't do anything on a whim. Why are you trying to connect Frank Shay to the hijacking?''

"A fraud investigator received a tip from one of Shay's former cell mates. The insurance company is convinced Shay got away with the money. If he stashed it on the ranch, it explains why he had a delivery van and why he went trigger happy.''

"Who rats out a cell mate to an insurance company? Why did the insurance people contact you? Why not the FBI?''

"I still haven't figured it out exactly,'' Carson said. "Something to do with finder's fees. To top it all off, we just recovered a body from the Shay house.''

"Homicide?''

"Looks like it.''

"Who's the victim?'' Paul asked.

"Don't know yet. Allegedly, two hijackers escaped with the money. Frank Shay and Deke Fry. Maybe Fry is our John Doe.''

"Hold on, I'm writing this down.''

"They left behind the ringleader at the plane. He was killing all the witnesses, including his accomplices. So Shay and Fry were running from the law *and* the ringleader. The snitch said Shay was scared.''

Paul snickered. "So Shay gets himself thrown into the slammer on purpose? He was hiding?''

Carson turned the idea over, looking for holes. There were plenty. He kept coming back, however, to the fact that from age twelve to the day he died, Frank Shay had spent more time inside penal institutions than out. Prison was familiar, even comfortable. He could have done three years without breaking a sweat.

Three years was long enough for the hijacking case to grow cold and for the ringleader to tire of looking for the men who had ripped him off.

"Can you find out who Shay's cell mates were during that last stint in Lewis?"

"I'll do one better, Carson. I shoot pool once a week with an FBI agent. He's a good old boy, for a fed. He can pull strings you and I can't even see."

Carson worried about Madeline. Bad enough she couldn't go back home, but half the town of Ruff was gunning for her and the other half was hoping the sheriff would arrest her. Every question he asked, every person he involved upped the risk of media involvement. If reporters got wind that Shay had buried thirty million dollars, all hell would break loose. Treasure hunters would swarm over the Shay ranch. People might think Madeline knew where the money was hidden.

"Can you hold off for a while, Paul? At least until we get some confirmation? I promised the insurance guy I'd protect his source. Do you have any contacts in Lewis?"

"A few. But you know nothing ticks off the feds faster than local yokels trespassing on their cases."

"If I get any hard evidence, I'm more than happy to dump it."

"Roger that. I'll get back to you."

Pete slapped both hands atop the desk and hoisted to his feet. "What in the world is going on?"

"Just between you, me and these walls, it's possible Frank Shay stole thirty million dollars and buried it on his ranch."

Pete looked ready to mop the floor with his chin. Carson almost laughed. He revealed Shay's possible role in the hijacking, including the part about Shay giving Madeline the ten grand, telling her he won the lottery.

"So that's why she turned up," Pete said. "Talk about winning the lottery."

Carson covered his eyes with a hand. "No, man, no. She's getting ready for an art show. She doesn't know about the hijacking."

"You sure?"

"Yes, I'm sure."

"What about the body under the house?"

"She doesn't know anything about that, either."

"So where did she take off to?"

Pete had been a cop for nearly thirty years and Carson's right-hand man for the past eight. He depended on Pete, and he trusted him. "My place. I don't want anyone to know."

Pete was pushing fifty, but his hair was shiny black without a trace of gray and his mahogany-colored face bore few wrinkles. His smile was boyish.

Carson drew his head aside. "What are you smirking at?"

"Madeline Shay is quite a looker. Pretty as a spotted pony at sunrise."

"I hadn't noticed," Carson lied. Heat crept over the back of his neck.

"Right."

"Can it, Pete. I'm keeping her safe until we catch the knuckleheads who tried to burn her up."

Pete scratched his head. "Guess it escaped my notice that you're one for putting up witnesses in your own house."

Wanda opened the door, again without bothering to knock. "That pesky salesman is back," she hissed. "Whatever he's selling, I hope you ain't buying."

"Send him in. Oh, and Wanda." He rapped the desk with his knuckles. "That's what I want to hear before I see your face next time."

She sniffed haughtily. "Spoken like a man who don't know how to do right by a woman."

Pete grimaced quizzically at the dispatcher's comment. Carson suspected Judy had spread her tale of woe. How long, he wondered, before Judy's story turned into a sordid tale of a perverted chief of police abusing an innocent housekeeper before turning her out into the cold, cruel world.

Bannerman entered the office. His suit, so crisp a few days ago, was wrinkled and limp. A purplish splotch stained his necktie. He recoiled from Pete and turned a pleading look on Carson that brought to mind a starving puppy. "Can I please have a word with you, Chief Cody?"

"Close the door, Mr. Bannerman. This is Sergeant Morales. I don't keep secrets from him."

"You promised!" If Bannerman had stamped his foot, the petulant child act would be complete.

"I promised to protect your source, sir. So far I'm doing that. Now have a seat."

Bannerman dropped onto a chair. He fiddled with his shirt cuffs and the buttons on his jacket. "You know why it is imperative that I keep my investigation quiet."

"Sergeant Morales won't run around the Shay ranch with a metal detector and a pickax."

"My job—"

Carson held up a hand. "The situation has changed. It is no longer possible for me to act as your liaison and guide. Did you see the newspaper? We found a body. If anyone does any digging at the Shay ranch, it'll be law officers, not you."

"I asked you to help for a very good reason," Bannerman said.

Carson thought the reason might be that Bannerman believed a small-town cop was greedy enough or stupid enough to keep a little matter like thirty million dollars just between the two of them. He wavered between feeling insulted and amused.

"I want the name of your informant," Carson said.

"I told you I don't know."

"You're lying, sir."

Bannerman puffed up and his eyes widened into moons. "Mutual Security and Assurance has policies," he said, as if invoking the name of his employer held special power.

"I don't care about your policies, sir. You can give me the name or you can give it to the FBI. Failure to do so could be construed as obstruction of justice."

Bannerman squirmed. "I don't know his name."

"If your company intends to give him a finder's fee, you can figure out who he is."

"Our policy—"

Carson slammed a fist on the desk. Bannerman jumped and cringed. "I don't give a damn about your policies! I've got dead people, major crimes. If you can't or won't cooperate, then you better find some muckety-muck in your company who will."

"Mutual Security and Assurance doesn't like threats." He lifted his pointy chin and resettled his eyeglasses with a prissy motion. His hands trembled. "We have lawyers."

"I have handcuffs and a jail cell." He beckoned with

his fingers. "Give me the name of your superior and I'll ask him."

"Don't you worry," Bannerman said. "You'll hear from him shortly. Good day."

Carson had a hunch he'd be hearing from a corporate attorney rather than an executive. It didn't matter. Paul Imagia could run down a name long before Bannerman spilled his guts. "Oh, and Mr. Bannerman, sir."

Bannerman opened the door, but he stood there, watching warily over his shoulder. "Yes?"

"You put one toe on the Shay ranch and I'll charge you with interfering with an investigation. Understand?"

Dark fury flashed behind the thick lenses of the little man's glasses. As long as Bannerman behaved himself, Carson didn't care.

The air in the office seemed cleaner after Bannerman had left. Carson hauled in a deep breath.

"What a pissant." Pete snorted. "Company policy, my sweet Maria. Are you scared?"

"Terrified."

"Hard to believe he's a fraud investigator. Pretty squirrelly."

"That's what he says."

"How much is the finder's fee?"

"Didn't ask. It doesn't matter. This office doesn't accept rewards."

"Ah, come on now, Chief. I can think of two old cowboys right off my head who have too many hard miles on their pickup trucks." Pete barked a loud laugh. "How would a person even start spending thirty million dollars?"

He sent Pete back to the Shay ranch to keep an eye on the investigation and help in guarding the crime scene. He busied himself with routine paperwork, but it was hard concentrating on parking violations and petty-theft complaints when his head was filled with death and destruction and trying to fit all the puzzle pieces that were Frank Shay into a coherent whole.

He went off duty at six o'clock. Once out of town he drove faster than usual. When he got stuck behind a tractor hauling a hay wagon, he drummed the steering wheel with his fingers and watched for an opportunity to pass. He was reaching for the siren when he realized how impatiently he was acting. It wasn't like him to hurry unless it was an emergency.

Eagerness transformed into dread when he approached the house and found it dark. The sun barely touched the mountain peaks. The sky mellowed to dusky blue and the shadows were heavy beneath the porch roof. Rosie pranced along the fence, snorting and tossing her head, foolish as a filly.

Carson stood for a while, listening. In the distance, crows traded cackling gossip and closer in, a cactus wren complained. Nothing seemed out of place. He unsnapped his pistol holster before he fit a key into the lock and opened the front door.

A savory, meaty scent wafted on cool air. His stomach growled so loudly he clapped a hand over it. The swamp cooler rumbled. The house was quiet and gloomy.

Eyes wide, ears straining, he crept to the kitchen.

The smell of roasting meat, rich and peppery, set his mouth to watering. A red pinpoint of light shone from the stove, indicating the oven was on. Madeline sat at the table, hunched over so her nose nearly touched her work, her hands deft and sure as she sewed beads.

The kitchen window faced due east. At this time of

the evening it may as well be night. Carson cleared his throat.

Madeline started. Her eyes were luminous. Her full lips parted.

She's a looker, Pete had said.

In the gloom, her bruises and cuts weren't obvious. What was obvious was the perfect oval of her face, the long, elegant line of her neck and the shining depths of her eyes. His breath caught in his suddenly thick throat. He grew aware of his own heartbeat.

For the life of him he couldn't figure out why he noticed. Jill was the love of his life, the only woman he had ever wanted, and she was gone, so there would be no more.

That didn't stop him from drinking in Madeline's smooth, honey-hued skin and imagining how that glossy black hair would slide between his fingers in a waterfall of silk. Trapped by a yearning he couldn't control, didn't want and could not deny, he was rendered useless.

"Oh," she said. "I didn't hear you come home."

Her voice brought him back to reality. He flipped the light switch.

Madeline blinked and looked around. A smile captured her entire face, making her eyes sparkle and creating a dimple in one cheek. "I can't believe how dumb I am! I forgot completely you have electricity."

"It's one of them newfangled inventions," he drawled. "Got me some runnin' water, too."

She wrinkled her nose in mock annoyance. "Let me slide the biscuits into the oven. The potatoes went bad, but I saw a box of instant mashed in the pantry. Will that do?"

"You making gravy?"

"I am."

"Then we have to have potatoes. Do I have time to change clothes and tend the mare?"

"Certainly."

When she pulled the roasting pan out of the oven and slid in the biscuits, he watched her slender hips and the graceful lines of her long arms. She could catch him staring like a schoolboy. He made his feet move. Delicious aromas followed him upstairs. His appetite was yelling like a Fourth of July shindig. This past year, eating had been like sleeping, something that needed doing, despite a lack of interest. Jill was a fair cook, but to her it was a chore the way yard work was a chore for him.

His mother was a terrific cook. For years she supplied restaurants in Ruff, Snowflake, Show Low and Springerville with fruit pies, quick breads and cinnamon rolls. Before Mom and Dad retired to Lake Havasu City, Jill had jumped at every invitation to eat at the senior Cody's house. Her favorite meal was OPC—other people's cooking.

He had changed clothes and gone outside to the barn before it occurred to him that he was reminiscing about Jill without hurting. He fed and watered Rosie. His belly growled so loudly, the mare flicked her ears. "If you were a carnivore, you'd understand," he told her before hurrying back to the house.

The roast beef was dark, so tender it fell apart at a touch. The carrots and onions were caramelized. Biscuits in a basket were golden brown, fat and flaky. A bowl of Three Sisters—beans, corn and squash—steamed. The only lumps in the gravy came from bits of meat and cracked pepper. Even the instant mashed potatoes looked good.

Madeline poured a big glass of iced tea and added a slice of lemon. She placed it on the table and a long strand of black hair unfurled over her shoulder. He squeezed his hands against his thighs, resisting the lure of her hair. She stood shyly a few feet from the table.

"Did you already eat?" He plucked a biscuit from the basket and slathered it with butter. *Don't look at her,* he warned himself. *Look at the food.*

"No."

"Then grab a plate and join me. Please."

She sat, but he soon figured out she wouldn't start until after he loaded his plate. She didn't move at all until he forked beef into his mouth and practically purred. It tasted even better than it smelled.

"Whoa, Nelly," he said. "I'm surprised some man hasn't roped you to his stove. This is incredible."

Smiling, she spooned Three Sisters onto her plate.

"You don't have a boyfriend to cook for?" As soon as the question slipped out, he wished to reel it back in. It sounded condescending and nosy. Worse, it made him sound interested. Which he was, but he didn't want to be and he sure didn't want her to know it.

She split a biscuit and drizzled it with honey. "I'm lousy at picking men. It's like I wear a sign saying Jerks Welcome Here. I'm better off putting my energy into art."

Her frankness flustered him. He focused on the food, which wasn't difficult since his mouth was celebrating.

"Nice thing about being Apache." She shrugged. "Half Apache anyway. We respect artists. I don't get pestered much about being single. No matter how much a white girl accomplishes, people look at her funny if she doesn't land herself a man."

He swallowed a piece of carrot so sweet it could be

sugared. "I miss being married." Embarrassed at speaking that particular thought aloud, he froze.

"Carson?"

He lifted his face and found those solemn green eyes regarding him.

"I know it's too hard for you...me being here. You have a good heart. Have to say you're a better man than I've ever known. So don't think for a minute I don't appreciate what you're trying to do, but I really have to go."

He wanted her to go. He wanted her to stay. How he'd gotten himself into this dilemma was the damnedest thing. He buttered another biscuit. Food helped him think, so he took seconds and seriously considered thirds.

Sheriff Gerald called. Carson left Madeline doing dishes in the kitchen while he took the phone into the front room.

"Sorry to bother you at home, Carson, but I just heard from the medical examiner."

"Do you have an ID on the body? Do you know how long it's been there? Man or woman?"

"No and no and it's male. M.E. says a small round hole at the base of the skull counts as a cause of death."

"Shot."

A coyote howled. It sounded so close Carson flipped on the porch light. He pulled aside a curtain and searched the darkness beyond the circle of light. Coyotes couldn't hurt Rosie, but they occasionally made her nervous enough to hurt herself.

"Eventually," Gerald said. "He was tortured first."

Carson dropped the curtain. "How does the M.E. know that?"

"Busted facial bones and shinbones. And, in the

M.E.'s technical jargon, finger bones snapped like sticks. I'm surprised you didn't hear the screaming. Wonder what made Shay do that to a man.''

Shay had thirty million reasons.

"Carson?'' Madeline asked from the hallway. "Would you like more iced tea?''

"Who was that?'' Gerald asked.

Carson pressed a finger to his lips and shot a warning look at her. She started, wide-eyed, and pressed a hand over mouth. She hurried back to the kitchen.

"Television.''

"Like hell! You son of a gun, you've got a woman up there.'' Gerald laughed. "It's about time. Who's the lucky lady? Or should I say, who's making you a lucky man?''

"Madeline Shay.''

Dead silence responded. Carson thought it served Gerald right for talking like a dirty old man.

"Nothing is going on between us. She needs a place to stay. Seeing how someone from Ruff tried to kill her, I consider it my duty to insure her safety.''

"I'd say that's carrying duty a mite too far. You're asking for trouble.''

"It's my job.'' He heard water running. "I know you don't believe the Shay connection to the Worldwide hijacking. But the evidence is piling up.''

"What evidence is that?''

He listened for Madeline again. He told the sheriff about the strange circumstances of Frank Shay's last stint in prison and the money Shay gave his daughter and the way he'd divorced his wife then boasted about winning the lottery. How the insurance company based their investigation on the word of a man who claimed to once share a cell with Shay. How the informant claimed Shay and another man escaped with the money, leaving a third behind with his murder victims.

"It's still crazy." Gerald didn't sound so blustery or confident.

"I've been talking with Paul Imagia. He's running down names for me. He doesn't think it's far-fetched."

"And you think Shay's girl will lead you to the money?"

"Not even close. She doesn't know anything."

"What makes you so sure? 'Cause of them long legs and big eyes?"

"You interviewed her last year. Did you ever for a second think of her as being involved in any way with her father or what he did?"

The sheriff took his time answering. "Apaches are harder to read than any Navajo. One-word answers and no facial expressions, shutting down when they don't want to talk."

Carson wanted an answer, not bigotry. His shoulders ached with growing tension. "Did you ever consider her as anything other than a routine interview?"

He made a harsh noise. "Her mama was a whole other rodeo! I plumb put her out of mind. Woman's a lunatic. She must have called me fifty times, accusing me of stealing Shay's money. I gave her a copy of the inventory to shut her up, but I finally had to get the tribal police to talk to her about harassment."

"He picked at her, telling her he'd won the lottery and she wasn't getting a penny of it," Carson said.

"Thumbing his nose at her. It doesn't prove he hijacked a plane."

"It doesn't prove he didn't." He heard an engine and looked out the window. Headlights broke the darkness.

"I've got company. Have the M.E. check the bones against a man named Deke Fry."

"He's missing?"

"I'm not positive he even exists. But if we get a match, we might have found ourselves a hijacker." The shape of a Jeep appeared from the darkness. "I gotta go. Call me if you hear anything."

Carson stepped onto the porch before Tony reached the door. His neighbor carried a six-pack of beer under one arm.

"What's the crime report today?" Tony popped a beer free from its plastic collar and handed it over.

Carson studied the can of imported beer. He drank too much when Tony came around. He rubbed his thumb in the icy condensation on the can. "Nothing to write home about."

"So who died? The newspaper didn't say if it was a man or a woman."

"I can't talk about an open investigation."

"You're rating a zero on the fun meter. How about Madeline? Would she like a beer?" He canted his head toward the door.

Carson's nerves jumped.

Tony hooted laughter and opened a beer. The can sighed and fizzled. "Holding out on me. I'm thinking you're a monk and here you've got the best-looking woman I've seen in these parts."

"What makes you think Madeline is here?"

"Ooh, a secret." Tony clucked his tongue. "Sorry about that, but don't worry, I'll never tell." Tony's smile lost steam and he backed a step. "Whoa, whoa, don't look at me like that. I was out for a run this morning when I saw her in the window."

Carson didn't know what to do first. Toss Tony off the porch or strangle Madeline. "What did she say?"

Tony shuffled his feet and glanced at the Jeep as if judging how long it would take to run for it. "You best go figure out where you dropped your sense of humor, man. Nothing happened. She didn't even let me in the house."

Carson chewed his inner lip, judging the depth of Tony's sincerity. Tony habitually ran where fancy took him and he trespassed with impunity on Carson's land. On the other hand, Madeline hadn't said a word. He breathed slowly a few times until certain he wouldn't erupt in anger.

"Madeline is in protective custody. It's not like I don't trust you, but in this situation I have to play it safe. Nobody can know she's here. It's a matter of life and death."

"Who am I going to tell?"

How about all those women you cat around with in Ruff?

Tony sobered, solemn for a change. "Do you think someone tried to burn Madeline? Deliberately?"

"It's possible."

"I'm sorry for fooling around. I don't mean anything. You know that, don't you?"

Carson popped the tab on the beer and lifted it to his lips. He managed half a smile. "Life is a little stressful right now."

"I understand. So how is she?"

"Okay. She's pretty tough."

"Would she like a beer?" he repeated.

Automatic refusal hovered on his tongue. Honesty, however, made him concede his reluctance to let Tony inside had less to do with protecting Madeline and far more with how attracted she was to jerks.

Chapter Seven

Madeline lifted her chin and folded her arms across her chest. She refused to allow Carson Cody to make her feel like a rebellious teenager. No harm, no foul was the way she saw it. He was being unreasonable.

"I'm a grown woman," she said. "I'd like to know what gives you the right to come in here grouching at me about something I have no control over."

From his post at the kitchen sink, he glowered at her. "Why didn't you tell me Tony had come by?"

"I did exactly what you told me to do. I didn't unlock the door. I didn't invite him in the first place."

"Why did you let him see you?"

She rolled her eyes. It was past her bedtime and she was tired. Tony was his friend and neighbor, but Carson acted as if she had helped Tony burglarize the house.

"Look," she said, "if the price of help is you treating me like a stupid kid then I don't want it."

He shut his mouth. His gaze drifted toward the back door. "I want you safe. I don't have the manpower to post a guard. I need your cooperation."

"Is Tony dangerous? Will he hurt me?"

"No." His big hands worked restlessly over his biceps.

"Will he run around telling everybody I'm here?"

He scratched his arms, tugged at the T-shirt sleeves. Lights danced in his hair and his face was shadowed. "No."

"Mind telling me why it's such a big deal then?"

"I guess it's not."

Oh, but it was a big deal to him. It didn't make sense to her and perhaps it didn't make sense to him, either. "I will stay away from the windows from now on."

"Okay," he muttered.

"I've been taking care of myself for a long time. I don't look for trouble and I do my best to not tempt fate." Not a particularly convincing argument considering how she had discounted the problems inherent with moving into her father's house. "I don't go into the basement when I suspect a monster is down there."

The corners of his mouth tipped into a rueful smile. "Okay."

"I overheard you telling Tony I didn't want company."

Tension returned and he shifted his stance, cocking a hip to take his weight. Madeline wanted to slap his hands to make him quit fidgeting.

"Tony must think I'm socially unacceptable."

He snapped up his head and those gray eyes were Arctic ice. "If you're so hot to see him I'll run you over to his place for a visit."

She flinched. Hot to see Tony? Where had that come from? Then she saw it in his piercing gaze that threatened to swallow her and the pained set of his mouth and the tension that set his fingers to digging at his own flesh and made the very atmosphere quiver. Carson was jealous.

She despaired over a rise of giddiness. His desire

came from pheromones, the instinctive allure of a feminine shape and the frustration of a man denied the comfort of a woman. It came from the animal part of him. His intellect knew her as Frank Shay's daughter. His heart would always be stone against her.

She tucked a strand of hair behind her ear. "Only thing I'm hot for is a pillow for my head. Good night, Carson."

"You don't want to watch television or something?" A surly offer at best.

"No, thank you." She gave her beadwork a lingering look, sorry to leave it for the night, but her hands were sore and she couldn't focus well enough to see the tiny holes in the beads. She went upstairs.

The house squeaked and creaked. The swamp cooler sounded as if it held conversations with itself, a mechanical language of rushes, whispers, thumping and chugs. Coyotes held a concert and crickets reported the time and weather. Behind closed eyelids, she saw Carson Cody. She felt the ghosts of his hands so tenderly ministering to her after the fire. She heard the sexy huskiness of his voice. The strength of those big arms.

She flung herself over and punched the pillow. "Sleep, damn it."

Light shone under the closed door. A shadow cut the thin rectangle of light. Self-disgust rose at how much she wanted Carson to pause, open the door, come sit beside her on the narrow bed. It relieved her when the shadow kept moving and the lights went off.

OVER THE NEXT FEW DAYS Madeline fell into a routine. Up at dawn to prepare breakfast for Carson and send him off to work. Bead all day. During breaks, dust the house and do laundry and run the vacuum cleaner.

Make dinner from the groceries Carson brought home. Clean the kitchen, bead some more while he retired to the front room to read the newspaper and watch television. Carson didn't offer personal information and she refrained from asking personal questions. Neither talked about the fire or the body. She stayed out of his way and he stayed out of hers. Reason said her attraction to him would cause trouble sooner than later.

If she weren't making such terrific progress on her bead projects she might heed reason.

On Friday, when he came home from work, he was in a mood. He laid a folded newspaper on the table, which he hadn't done before. He didn't make appreciative noises about the meal.

"Sheriff finished with the crime scene."

"What does that mean?" She passed him a roasted sweet potato. "Do you know who set the fire?"

"It means the forensics boys have collected all the evidence they can find. It means you can go back if you've a mind to. And yes I know who set the fire, but I can't prove it. Yet."

He believed Matt and Sug Harrigan had set her house on fire. Their uncle, Maurice, mayor of Ruff, swore the boys were with him at the time of the fire. Unless the forensics experts found hard evidence proving otherwise, the sheriff had to accept the alibi.

"I see." She took the smallest pork chop. "So if I want, I can set up camp, and go back to working in the garage. You said yourself the well and pump are okay."

He set the thickest pork chop on his plate. "You're not going back there. You'd be isolated, no way to buy groceries or get help if you hurt yourself."

That he'd missed her facetious tone seemed a poor omen. "No, I'm not going back there. I've been thinking. When taxes are due next year, I'm not paying them. The county can have the ranch and good riddance. It's brought me nothing but heartache."

"Have you thought of somewhere to go?"

He wanted her gone.

"I have a friend, Nona Redhawk, who lives on the reservation. She's isolated enough that I don't have to worry about running into anybody. I can do for her around her house and studio to pay my keep. She's gone right now, but she'll be back soon." She didn't want to say Nona was on a lecture tour and wouldn't return home until June.

He shook his head. "The reservation isn't safe."

"If you want to get rid of me why are you telling me every place is unsafe?"

"I'm not trying to get rid of you."

"You'll miss my cooking?" When he didn't crack a smile, she touched his hand and waited until he looked at her. "Something is wrong. What is it?"

"You realize there are two active investigations going on. Arson and homicide. The only connection is location and the fact that the arson revealed the homicide."

"Okay," she said, stretching out the word while wondering what this had to do with her.

"Have you ever heard of a man named Deke Fry?"

She didn't need to think about it. "I don't know anybody named Deke."

"The M.E. managed to put the name to the body. He was tortured before he was killed with a bullet in the head."

She put down her fork. "One of my father's prison buddies?"

"It appears they met outside prison."

"My father killed him?"

"We may never know. The FBI is retracing Fry's steps, trying to establish time of death."

"FBI? I thought the sheriff was investigating."

He ate a bite of pork, stalling. He drew a deep breath and unfolded the newspaper. He placed it on the table so she could read the headline story.

Sixth and Seventh Hijackers? Two photographs of men. One she didn't recognize, the other was her father's broad Irish face glowering from a mug shot. An adjoining photograph showed a 727 jet, sporting a Worldwide Parcel logo, with the cargo and passenger doors wide-open. It was grounded on what appeared to be an endless sea of sand.

She snatched up the newspaper and shook it flat to read the story that took up nearly three-quarters of the page and continued inside. It laid out how four criminals circumvented airport security, with the help of a Worldwide Parcel pilot, and boarded a jet carrying thirty million dollars in cash from Las Vegas casinos. They hijacked the plane and landed it on a salt flat in Utah. They murdered the airplane's crew, including the pilot who had helped them, and turned on each other. Five hijackers were shot to death. The money was never recovered.

According to official sources, new evidence linked Francis Brawley Shay III and Deacon Wesley Fry to the hijacking. The story rehashed what had happened on Crossruff Creek a year ago. It covered the fire at the ranch. The burned body was identified as Fry. Her name jumped from the page and her heart raced. The story said she had disappeared. Her mother, Cora Shay, was quoted, "Frank said he hit the lottery and made sure I didn't get a penny of it. Ha! I should have figured it was from a robbery. Gave everything to that no-good daughter of his.''

She folded the newspaper neatly. Carson finished eating. She barely touched her plate and didn't care to. ''Is that where the ten thousand dollars came from?''

''Possible.''

Hurt arced through her midsection. ''If you knew about this, why didn't you tell me?''

''Because all I had was Bannerman's say-so and no evidence.'' He tapped the newspaper. ''I don't know who leaked this. I've never heard of this reporter, Nick Iola. Now that the story is out, there's no going back, especially since this made national news. It doesn't take a brain surgeon to make the connection between thirty million dollars and a deserted ranch as the perfect place to hide it.''

It hit her what he meant and she gasped. ''My father buried thirty million dollars? That's not possible. Oh! What if it burned up?''

''Investigators would have found some trace of it.''

''I never really checked the back rooms. There were so many mice I worried about snakes and hantavirus.''

''Trust me, if thirty million dollars was laying around the house, someone would have found it long before the fire.'' He pushed the plate away and leaned forward, resting his arms on the table. His forearms were corded with muscle and burned dark by the sun. He smiled and for a moment concerns about hijackings and money and her father disappeared. The entire world focused on how the lines in his forehead eased and his eyes sparkled with warmth.

Her belly thumped a warning.

''An anonymous tipster told Bannerman that Shay buried the money before he went to prison. The insurance company is offering a finder's fee to whoever helps them recover the money. I suspect Bannerman is back in Las Vegas concocting some kind of lawsuit to force your cooperation.''

''Oh, great.'' She sighed. ''Just what I need.''

''Seems to me if the money is buried on your land, you ought to be the one to find it.''

''What am I supposed to do with thirty million dollars?''

He stared, for a moment befuddled, his lips parted. He burst into laughter. A hearty, booming laugh that echoed against the tall ceiling. Madeline bristled at being the butt of a joke at the same time a warm tingling spread through her torso, loosening her hips and knees.

His laughter trailed off, leaving his chest hitching. He swiped at an eye with a knuckle.

''What's so funny?''

''I don't know. You are. I doubt there's another human being in this whole damned country who'd have said what you said.''

''Well pardon me,'' she said tartly.

''You're not supposed to keep the money. You turn it over to the insurance company and they pay you the finder's fee.''

''Oh.'' She chewed her lower lip. ''Really?''

''Getting their money back will have those insurance folks dancing in the streets. I imagine they'll be generous.''

''How generous?''

''Reckon it's easy enough to find out.''

She didn't need much. Beads and beading supplies were her biggest expense, and she had enough to finish her projects for the show. Two or three thousand dollars would pay rent and buy food through the summer. For a few thousand more she might be able to replace her van.

"So if I let Mr. Bannerman search the ranch, he'll pay me?"

"You find it. I have a problem with a jailbird getting everything. At least part of the reward should go to you."

The ranch spread out over hundreds of acres of rocks, scrub, prickly pear cactus and snakes. She wouldn't know where to begin looking. Besides which, the more she thought about it the less she wanted anything to do with stolen money.

"You don't seem very enthusiastic," he said.

"Even if I wanted a case of heatstroke digging in those hills, profiting from my father's crime turns my stomach."

"It's got nothing to do with profit. And like I said, it won't take long before folks figure out the ranch is a good place to start looking. Your land will be crawling with treasure hunters. Finder's fees bring out the pros, too."

"Pros?"

"Bounty hunters. Folks who make their living recovering stolen goods."

She laughed absently. Her world was so narrow.

"There's one small problem."

Her life was a series of problems, small and otherwise. "What's that?"

"Some think you knew about the money all along. That you conspired with your father."

Hurt rushed in. First her mother and now Carson. Her face froze in an impassive mask. Her shoulders and spine straightened.

Carson cocked an eyebrow. "That bothers you."

"Of course it does," she said, putting ice in her voice. When he kept quiet and the silence felt like a void, she added, "I get sick of being blamed for things I don't do. Maybe that's why people turn into criminals. As long as they're getting slammed for being related to drunks and whores and thieves, they might as well be what everybody thinks they are."

"If I thought you were involved, you wouldn't be sitting at my table."

She studied his pale eyes and suntanned face, seeking any sign of a lie. He sat still for her perusal, his gaze steady. "It means a lot you saying that," she said quietly.

"I'm not worried about law enforcement or the insurance company going after you. I've been on the phone with the FBI. They know you're here, they know your story, and they don't consider you a suspect. My worry is there could be an eighth hijacker."

"The paper said there were seven. Why do you say eight?"

"Bannerman says so. Shay was scared of the ringleader. He was supposed to die in Utah, but he got away. If true, he might come looking for you."

A frisson of fear ripped down her spine. Then came anger. She lived an honest, sober life, refusing to fall into the trap of booze and hopelessness that ruined so many lives on the reservation. She learned young to keep to herself, to not arm potential enemies with insights into her vulnerabilities. She'd never been arrested—never had so much as a speeding ticket. By virtue of being her father's daughter, and no other reason, she'd been burned out and now risked being stalked by a killer.

What was the point of being good?

"I'm not trying to spook you." He laid his hand atop hers.

"I am spooked!" She jerked her hand away. "All I want is to be left alone. I never asked for any of this."

"The sooner the money is found, the sooner you can put this behind you." He rose. "With the weekend and all I doubt anyone who knows anything about the finder's fee is working. I'll give the company a call on Monday."

There was nothing more to say. She cleared the table.

"I'm going to watch some TV. Might be something on the news."

Washing dishes, she couldn't put Carson from her mind. Maybe the money was the reason Carson had helped her. She doubted the town of Ruff paid him what he was worth. It felt funny thinking of him as a mercenary, but at least it let her know exactly where she stood.

MADELINE SLID the coffee cake into the oven. The kitchen was plain, functional, but pure luxury to her. If the beads hadn't called to her, she might have become a baker or chef.

She heard Carson moving around the house earlier. She guessed he was out in the barn. Last night she had thought about what he said. She knew how to reward his kindness and pay her debt.

Madeline entered the barn in time to see Carson pick up a baseball cap, slap it against his thigh and settle it on his head. He shoved the neck of the black mare. She turned a playful circle in the spacious stall. When he pushed a pitchfork into a pile of soiled straw, the mare snatched the cap and shook it the way a puppy shook a toy.

Madeline clapped her hands and laughed.

"Darned old horse thinks she's a pet dog," he said. He retrieved his cap and shooed the mare outside. He closed the half door.

Madeline watched the horse amble across the corral to a water trough. Tall and leggy with a long, elegant neck, she was friendlier than any horse Madeline knew. "Is she a Thoroughbred?"

"Through and through. Back in the day she was a hell of a jumper."

Madeline rested her arms on the stall door. Carson resumed cleaning.

"Hard to picture you on a jumping horse," she said.

"Hard for you, impossible for me. I prefer horses with sense enough to keep their feet on the ground. Rosie is Jill's horse." His eyes turned distant and sad. "Jill competed in show jumping and man oh man, she and Rosie were a pretty pair. Rosie all decked out in red ribbons and her tack gleaming like wax. Jill wearing a velvet jacket with her grandma's cameo at her throat."

"I saw the photographs of her. She was beautiful."

Muscles swelled in his jaw and his throat worked. He jammed the pitchfork into the dirt floor. Eyes blank, so stiff his arms and legs seemed made of iron, he pushed open the stall door and strode past Madeline. The door slapped against the wooden post and the latch clattered but didn't close. Madeline watched him leave the barn, walking fast, and knew she'd said too much.

She fastened the latch then headed back to the house to finish breakfast.

She found him in the kitchen. He rested a hand on the edge of the sink and held a glass of water. His eyes were red. He looked the way he had looked that day on Crossruff Creek, as if hoping lightning would strike him dead. She knew of no apology big enough, sincere enough to ease his pain. She had never let herself love anyone enough to feel that much pain over loss. She couldn't begin to imagine how terrible he must feel.

She pulled a package of bacon from the refrigerator and a skillet from under the stove. She needed to get out of here.

The bacon began to sizzle. The oven timer buzzed. She opened the oven door. The coffee cake was nicely browned.

"I never talk about her." He poured a cup of coffee. He looked puzzled. "I want to. I want to remember her. I want others to remember. But it hurts."

She focused on turning bacon strips. "I imagine so."

"First month or so after it happened I was numb. No thoughts in my head, no feelings in my heart. Just numb. It was like all the sound was sucked out of the air. Everything was gray. When it hit home, everything hurt. Everything reminded me that Jill was never coming back. I want to remember the good things, but it makes the hurting start all over again."

Madeline wished for the power to heal his heart.

She finished making breakfast in silence. They ate in silence. He returned to the barn. She cleaned the kitchen then sat down to work. Sorrow weighed her mind. Black wasn't really the color of sorrow, she decided. Sorrow was brown, parched like the desert. Fiery red for the rage over unwarranted loss. Deep, dark, muddy blue like a weary heart too worn-out to beat. A hunched shape formed, low and closed, shutting out the world, trying to fold upon itself, to make as small a target as possible for the pain.

Unable to concentrate on the phoenix, she rummaged through her supplies for a sketchbook. With quick pencil strokes, she drew a sad little demon with dull eyes, its spines limp from being battered, its skin pocked with neglected sores. She brought out her colored pencils.

She searched for hope. A ray of sunshine, a touch of faith, the tiniest promise that pain wasn't forever.

At the sound of a woman's voice, she nearly jumped out of her skin. Breath lodged in her throat like a ball of cement. Pencils clattered on the tabletop.

"Carson? I brought some groceries. We need to talk."

A blond woman, holding several plastic grocery bags, stopped in the doorway to the kitchen. Her eyes went so wide the whites showed all the way around the irises. Her mouth formed a shocked *O*. She looked from Madeline to the side of the sink where dishes were drying to the plate of coffee cake squares covered with plastic wrap.

The blonde sucked in a breath. "Who the hell are you?"

Rude, Madeline thought and clamped her lips to keep from making a comment. It hadn't occurred to her that Carson had a woman. It was tough to imagine, though, he found this angry creature attractive. She looked too young for him. She wore a very short denim skirt and a white blouse knotted so her belly showed. Her hair was teased and her makeup looked more suitable for a nightclub than for a grocery delivery.

"Hello?" the woman said sarcastically, implying Madeline wasn't merely not where she belonged, she was stupid, too. "What are you doing in Carson's house?"

"I'm visiting."

The woman narrowed her eyes, peering at Madeline

as if through a microscope. "Are you a cousin or something?"

Madeline didn't like this woman's suspicious tone, didn't like her questions and most especially didn't like her proprietary air. The woman waited a beat for Madeline to answer, then sniffed and swished across the floor to deposit the grocery bags on the counter nearest the refrigerator. She tottered on strappy sandals as if she never wore such high heels. The way she put the food away spoke clearly of her familiarity with the kitchen.

She whirled about and pointed a finger at Madeline. Her gasp was practically a shriek. "Oh my God! It's you!"

The back screen door slammed and Carson strode inside. He came to an abrupt stop. His shoulders were rigid. He clenched and unclenched his hands. "What are you doing here?"

The woman gaped in horror at Madeline. "I don't believe she's here. In your house!"

"Listen up now, Judy, this isn't what you think."

"Everybody knows she's the reason your wife got shot!"

Carson grabbed Judy's shoulders. She tensed up, her face scrunched and fearful. "Damn it, Judy, you shouldn't have come here."

Her chin quivered. "I—I guess I made a mistake."

"Yes, you did. Now you're going to fix it, understand?"

She nodded, but to Madeline it looked less like agreement and more like terror.

"No one, not your mother or your daddy or the preacher, absolutely no one can know Madeline is here. It is a matter of life and death. Do you understand?"

"Yes," Judy whispered.

Madeline stood. "Carson, you're scaring her. Please stop."

He let go and she staggered on those ridiculous shoes.

"I'm sorry for scaring you, Judy." He stared into her face until the blonde nodded. "It is very important that you understand. Madeline is in protective custody. If you go telling people she's here then I'm going to have to break the town budget in order to give her a police guard. That would be a bad thing, but not nearly as bad as letting someone hurt her because you can't keep your mouth shut."

Judy swallowed hard and nodded.

"Seeing how you're the only one who knows she's here, if word gets out I'll know who told. I will charge you with endangering a witness."

"I won't tell," Judy whispered.

"I'll walk you out." He gave Madeline a worried look as he took the blonde's elbow and walked her out of the kitchen.

Madeline picked up a pencil but couldn't stop listening. A car door slammed and the engine revved. A few moments later he returned to the kitchen. He scrubbed his hands in the sink.

"I'm sorry," Madeline said. "I didn't mean to cause trouble with your girlfriend."

Carson groaned. "She is *not* my girlfriend."

Judy sure looked and acted like a girlfriend.

"She kept house for me. I let her go. If she opens her big mouth…"

"Did you fire her because of me?"

He plucked bits of straw from his T-shirt. "No." His ears turned red.

"You did, didn't you?"

"She's a lousy cook." He heaved a long breath.

"Okay, I did fire her because of you." He clapped a hand to his forehead. "God, I didn't mean to scare her, but I hope I did. Judy Green is the worst gossip in the whole county."

Chapter Eight

Madeline jabbed the pencil at her sketch. She had to get out of this house, get out of Carson's life before she destroyed him. Maybe Nona would let her live in her house until she returned from her tour. Nona Redhawk was revered on the reservation, deemed one of the finest artists the Apache tribe had ever produced. No one bothered Nona's property—it was treated as sacred land. One light pencil tic gave the sorrow-demon a hint of a smile. She wished she could do the same for Carson. He slumped on a chair, his nose practically in his coffee cup, giving new meaning to the word "bummed."

She stretched an arm across the table and touched Carson's hand. "I am so sorry I got you into this."

To her bemusement, he smiled. "Not a person living can make me do anything I don't want to do. I'm glad you're here."

His words were so warm her fierce determination to leave faded. A warning thumped her belly.

"Do you have some kind of form I can sign that gives you permission to search the ranch? I want you to find the money. You keep the finder's fee."

He sat straighter and cocked his head.

"I mean it. Considering all the bad luck the ranch has brought me I can only imagine what would happen with the finder's fee."

He laid a big hand over hers. His palm was pleasantly rough. "Jill was an artist of sorts. Weaving wool and making her own dyes and such. She was nutty, too. I guess it's an artist thing."

She had no idea what he meant, but who cared when his hand was warm atop hers. His gray eyes locked with hers. His smile was a treasure. "You're saying I'm nutty?"

"Yes, ma'am, I am. No such thing as curses. Money is just money."

"I never said a word about curses. I mean, well, you know what I mean. It can't be a good thing to profit from my father's crimes. It would bug me. I'd rather you had it. It seems right that way."

His thumb stroked the tender inside of her wrist. He didn't seem aware he was doing it, but she was more than aware—she was alive with the sensation.

"Then we have a problem. As an officer of the law I can't accept monetary gifts, rewards or bounties."

"Oh." The sensation of his absent caress was snaking up her arm and getting perilously close to her heart. She gently withdrew her hand. "I guess that leaves Mr. Bannerman."

"Or the FBI. If they find it, nobody gets a reward. You need the money."

"That's not the point."

"Before you decide, let's find out what the finder's fee actually is."

"No amount of money will change my mind."

"Let's check anyway." He nodded at the empty coffee cup beside her sketch pad. "How about a fresh pot?"

"I can do that."

"Keep working. Coffee is one thing I never screw up."

She didn't need to be told twice to go back to the beads. She finished a row and had started another when he gave her a fresh cup of coffee. He stood behind her, studying her sketch of sorrow.

"That's one sad sack of a critter if I ever saw one."

"He's supposed to be."

"Good drawing. May I?"

She hated showing her sketches. They were too rough, too raw and too personal, going straight from her soul through her fingers and onto the pages. Hoping he changed his mind, she nodded ever so slightly. He picked up the book. She appreciated how he held the edges, as if aware that the oil from his fingers could transfer to the pages. He leafed through the drawings, his expression impassive.

Unable to stand it, she held out a hand. "They're just doodles. Fooling around to help me think."

"If these are doodles, I'd like to see when you're serious. They're incredible."

She listened for mockery. Braced for the "but."

"Do you paint pictures along with beading?"

"I have."

"Hope I can see them someday." He gave back the sketchbook. "Be an honor."

The eager, needy child within wriggled at his praise. The sensual woman, weary of being shoved to the far reaches, flexed her muscles and made herself known along every nerve path. "I'd be honored to show you. Someday." It was too hard looking at him straight on.

She'd spontaneously combust. She lowered her eye-lashes and turned her head. She peeked sideways. His mobile brow raised. She felt every molecule of air in her chest. Her heartbeat pulsed against her eardrums.

He took a step back. His chest hitched. A slight action and quick, but she noticed. Just as she noticed how he smelled of sunshine, sweet hay and horses.

He raked a hand through his hair. He rested the hand on the back of his neck. "There's repairs on the porch I need to get to. If you'd like to bring your beads out there and keep me company, I wouldn't mind."

Oh, Madeline, she thought, don't do this. Do not melt beneath his gaze. Do not dream of his body pressed against yours. Do not imagine, for even one second, that one iota of good could come from a physical relation-ship with this man.

"Okay," she said.

He struck a chair with his hip, caught it before it fell, and practically ran out of the kitchen.

MADELINE RAN A DUSTING CLOTH over framed photo-graphs atop the fireplace mantle.

Carson had gone to town early to buy Sunday papers. Her father and the hijacking were still front-page news. One story quoted her mother extensively, saying Frank and Madeline were tight as ticks and the only reason he turned to a life of crime was to lavish his spoiled daugh-ter with luxuries.

The telephone rang. Carson answered, hung up and it rang again. His voice grew increasingly impatient with reporters and townsfolk.

"Madeline," he yelled. "The timer dinged. Want me to pull out the biscuits?"

"I'll get it." She glanced at a photograph of Carson

and Jill wearing formal clothing. Jill looked as if someone had told a ribald joke and she was doing her best not to laugh. With a hand on his pretty wife's shoulder, Carson stood tall and proud.

She hurried to the kitchen.

"You don't have to clean up around here." He had the *Arizona Republic* spread out on the table. "You aren't the housekeeper."

"I don't mind." She pulled biscuits from the oven. "It's my fault you let Judy go."

The telephone rang again. Carson snatched it up. "Chief Cody." He listened and rolled his eyes, and his mouth twitched as if he fought an outburst.

"Any sightings are a hoax. Don't even bother wasting paper to write them down. Got it? Out." He put down the phone with such exaggerated care Madeline knew he wanted to pound it to pieces. "Can you believe it? Some idiot reported seeing you headed south on Highway Sixty driving a brand-new Ford Explorer."

He abruptly pushed away from the table, snatched up the phone and stomped out of the kitchen.

When he returned, he said, "I don't know how to keep people off your property. I don't have enough manpower for a patrol. Best I can do is post No Trespassing signs then actually prosecute anybody we catch. Can you hear the traffic on Hoshonee? Sounds like an interstate down there."

"I hate causing trouble."

"You aren't. *They* are. Is breakfast ready? I'm hungry enough to eat bear on the hoof."

She didn't understand. He didn't strike her as the stubbornly stupid type. Maybe protecting her was some sort of twisted penance. Punishment for losing his wife.

If so, it was unhealthier than the stupidest stubbornness. After eating, she asked to borrow the telephone.

He jerked a thumb over his shoulder. "Have to plug in the base unit first. Unplug it when you're done. It rings again and my head will explode."

In the front room she paced and dusted and straightened bric-a-brac and wall pictures until the clock ticked past nine o'clock. Myriad reasons to not call crowded her head and weakened her nerve.

She wasn't brave, but knew how to pretend, knew how to steady her quaking voice and act calm.

She called Uncle Willy's house, praying he answered. Aunt Alma said, "Hello," and Madeline's heart sank. "Hello? Hello!"

"Hi, Aunt Alma, it's Madeline. May I speak to Uncle Willy?"

"Madeline Shay!" Alma made it sound like a curse. "You got some nerve calling here. You take all that money from my poor husband, food right out of my children's mouths, then you don't pay back nothing."

Madeline bit back rising fury. She had worked her tail off at the trading post and done it for minimum wage. On her own time, at her own expense, she ran errands and cleaned the store after hours. Aunt Alma resented having to pay family any wages at all.

"Please, may I speak to Uncle Willy?"

"It's in all the papers and on the television. I thought that worthless mother of yours was just talking crazy like she always does, but even a crazy woman has to be right sometimes. And you! You don't even think about your poor uncle and all his hungry children. No. You are a bad, selfish, spiteful girl, Madeline Shay. A bad, *bad* girl."

"Aunt Alma, that's a lie! I—"

Alma hung up, leaving Madeline with a silent telephone and a red cloud burning her eyes.

She resumed pacing and straightening and fuming. Uncle Willy probably knew Nona Redhawk's itinerary and how to contact her. He was the only person who might give her the benefit of the doubt.

She punched in Uncle Willy's number. "Please answer, please answer," she begged him. Alma answered again, her querulous voice sharp. Madeline hung up.

Hoping against hope, she called the trading post. Sometimes Willy did paperwork and stocked the shelves on Sundays. The phone rang and rang and rang. Conceding defeat, she hung up.

The telephone rang. Caller ID said Morales, Pedro. She carried the ringing phone to Carson.

"I think it is Sergeant Morales," she said.

Looking wary, he answered.

Madeline washed dishes. All Carson said was an occasional "uh-huh" and "no kidding," but he often looked her way. Her curiosity clamored.

Carson said, "I'll talk to her and get back to you." He hung up.

"Talk to me?" she asked. "About what?"

"The FBI wants to exhume your father's body. They can get an order from the court, but out of respect for the family, they prefer asking permission. You're the only person who can give it."

She was horrified. "Dig him up? From his grave? Why?"

"DNA evidence. The FBI can account for all the blood taken from the hijacked plane. Except for one sample. They eliminated the airplane crew, the dead hijackers and Deke Fry. They even eliminated mechanics who worked on the plane."

She groped for and found the clumsy locket. She clutched it through her shirt. She had zero respect for her father alive, but dead? Disrespect for the dead went against everything she believed. "I don't know."

"It's important evidence." He grimaced in apology. "They'll do it whether or not you grant permission."

"If they eliminate him, does that mean he wasn't one of the hijackers?"

"Not necessarily. You have a right to be there when the coffin is opened."

"Absolutely not!" She hugged herself.

"This is very important. Your permission will save time. This mess will end sooner."

"Do I have to talk to the FBI?"

"Pete will handle the paperwork. All you need to do is sign your name. Okay?"

God forgive me…Daddy forgive me. "Okay."

Carson patted the table. "Have a seat. The FBI is questioning anyone Shay might have talked to in Lewis. Far as I know, they've come up with zip. Did he ever mention names in his letters?"

Madeline lifted her gaze to the ceiling. "I didn't read his letters." Her cheeks warmed. "But I kept them."

Carson arched a brow.

Heat suffused her face and neck. The last time she talked to her father she had been seventeen years old. Her mother had been involved with a man who pounded on Cora, and considered Madeline fair game, too. The men fought, putting Cora's boyfriend in the hospital. Frank had promised to take Madeline away—off the reservation, out of Arizona, far away from the craziness of home. She had packed her meager belongings and spent an entire night seated on a concrete bench outside the Dairy Queen. He never showed.

"I'll get them," she said, unable to meet his eyes.

In the small room where she slept and stored her belongings, she crouched before the Dumb Stuff box. As a child the only thing she had ever wanted was for her mother to choose her daughter over alcohol and for her father to come home every night.

At thirty-one years old she still wanted it.

She carried the box downstairs and set it on the table. Wordlessly she watched him open the flaps. He picked up a mouse carved from wood.

"I didn't cry when he died. I didn't feel anything at all."

Carson brought out a pen-and-ink drawing of a little girl whirling in a joyous dance, her long black braids swinging.

"He let me down, deserted me, let my mother and her boyfriends abuse me." She sighed, her heart heavy. "And yet, even knowing he's a bad man, I had to believe…something."

Carson took her hand. She squeezed his fingers.

"He called me his little Indian princess. He never laid an angry hand on me." She lowered a sad gaze on the box. "That box holds the only good things he ever did."

She went outside to sweep the porch. She swept the floor, the windowsills and wooden chairs. She swept cobwebs from beneath the eaves until her shoulders ached, but the pain inside continued to gnaw. She tore dead vegetation out of flowerpots. There was nothing to plant. She gathered rocks, juniper twigs with interesting twists and whorls, bits of rusty wire, and dried grasses and weeds. She found wild turkey feathers and the wing of a scrub jay.

A shed snakeskin startled her. She looked around nervously for its owner. She used a stick to pick up the topaz-colored skin, which was dried and brittle, mostly intact. It crackled when she touched it with a finger. Not far away she found the molt of a grasshopper, tiny and perfect right down to the antennae and hairs on the legs. She created tiny landscapes in the pots.

The screen door squeaked. "What in the world are you doing?"

Her handiwork lined the porch railing. The whimsical deserts in miniature and arrangements of feathers and weeds tickled her. "I hope you don't mind. The plants were dead."

He looked as if he couldn't believe his eyes. "How do you do that? How do you even think it up? Art out of junk. Amazing."

Pleased, she grinned. "I have no idea."

"I'm impressed no matter how you do it." He glanced over his shoulder at the house. "He was surprisingly literate."

"Guess he did a lot of reading in prison."

"Why didn't you read the letters?"

She touched the locket, his final gift to her. "After the box of money, I couldn't take any more. I had to stop torturing myself. Did you learn anything?"

"A lot of talk about winning the lottery and the two of you starting over. Complaints about prison food." He displayed a small key. "This."

"What's it for?"

"According to his letter, it fits a locker at the bus station in Phoenix."

She covered her mouth with a hand. "The money! Oh my God, I had it all along?"

He laughed. "Not inside a luggage locker. Besides, it's been four years. It must be cleared out by now."

"Oh."

"We'll let the FBI handle it. Are you absolutely certain you never met Deke Fry?"

"Positive."

"Deke Fry was going to ask you for a favor. Your father wanted you to give Fry what he asked for, no questions asked. In exchange he promised to build you a house and a studio and buy all the art supplies you could ever want."

"What kind of favor?"

Carson shrugged. "Didn't say."

"I was traveling to shows when he was released from prison."

"He sure was anxious to hook up with you. He sent quite a few drawings. Your face was his favorite subject."

Emotion pinched her lungs. She was a sucker for her father's art. He used her weakness to manipulate her. "That's Daddy. Dangle a bit of hope in front of me and when I jumped, snatch it away."

"Any ideas about the favor?"

She puffed her cheeks and blew a long breath. "The ten thousand dollars? Or maybe he stashed something at Mama's house. He wouldn't dare ask Mama for anything, not after the way he divorced her." She added in a mutter, "Arrogant ass, thinking I'd help him and his thug friends."

"You have to give the letters to the FBI."

She didn't want to let go of the letters any more than she wanted to keep them. Both options hurt. She rearranged some stones in a pot to a more pleasing shape.

"You know, Madeline," he said, his voice so tender it soothed her anxiety, "I hang on to things that hurt me. I don't know why I do it, either."

CARSON STOOD in the doorway to the bedroom he had once shared with his wife. The walls were covered with family photos and weavings Jill had crafted from wool she sheared, spun and dyed. The carved maple furniture had been a wedding gift from his in-laws.

He waited for the tension in his chest to ease. Only stuff, he reminded himself—inanimate wood and metal and cloth.

Madeline appeared at the top of the stairs. "Did you call me?"

"Would you do me a favor?"

"Sure."

"I should have done it long ago, but, you know, procrastination and all. Would you clear out my wife's closet and drawers? It's a shame, her clothes going to waste when others can use them."

She peered between his shoulder and the doorjamb. Her hair was inky black and smelled of sunshine. He stepped into the room.

"You don't have to if you don't want to," he said.

"It's the least I can do. Are you all right with this?"

He waited for the ache to ease in his throat. "It needs doing."

A strange expression, a little wary and a whole lot puzzled, captured her face.

"Something wrong?"

She shook her head. "I am honored to help you."

She was a proud woman. He didn't want her thinking he considered her pitiful. "I'm donating everything to the church ladies' thrift shop. Feel free to take what you need. That way there's less for me to tote into town."

In his peripheral vision he glimpsed her tug the top button of the shirt she had worn since the fire. He felt stupid for not offering fresh clothing.

"There are some cartons out in the barn. I'll fetch them."

When he turned for the door, she blocked the way. Her calm eyes arrested him. "Why are you doing this?"

"Everybody says I should." He frowned at the dusty quilt on the bed. "The preacher, the guys at work, even Tony says it's important to clear—"

"I understand that," she interrupted. "I mean me. Why are you helping me?"

He hadn't a clue how to answer.

"When I saw you at Crossruff Creek, I was positive you meant to run me off. When you brought that man to look for the money, I was sure that was it. But no, you took my side. You saved my life. You took me into your home. Why not lock me up in protective custody? Save yourself the grief."

He swallowed hard and studied his boots.

"People either want to hurt me or use me. I avoid the first and handle the second."

"I'm not either of those."

"Are you sure?" She looked around the room. "Are you using me to hurt yourself?"

There might be an element of truth in what she said, even if he didn't want to admit it. "I'm not going to hurt you and I don't want anything from you. Except your cooking, which is real good." He hooked his thumbs in his pocket and shifted from foot to foot.

Her rigid shoulders and defiant eyes suggested she was as uncomfortable with this conversation as he was. "Doesn't it make you sick to look at me?"

"I thought I hated you. I thought I *should* hate you. You aren't your father. You're not responsible for what he did." He shrugged. "Fact is, I like you." He almost said how much he liked looking at her, how much he wanted to hold her and kiss her, but managed restraint.

She ducked her head and lowered her eyelids. Her shy, sideways look blew rational thought from his head. She tugged the hem of her shirt. Her hands were elegant, with long fingers and short nails. Fabric molded over her breasts. There was nothing boyish about her slender figure then. A small voice of reason—very small—told him he tread dangerous waters, but he brushed his fingertips lightly along the seam of the shirt. He longed to feel the texture of her skin.

Her almond eyes narrowed; her stare pierced him. When she lifted her face, he kissed her.

A light kiss, more of a caress of lips against lips. Touching her reminded him how much he loved the smell of a woman, how much he missed a woman's softness. His skin tightened, itching all over in sudden hunger. He clenched his hands, forcing them to remain at his sides. He didn't close his eyes, neither did she, and he saw flecks of gold within the green.

She touched his hand with hers, tentatively, as if in question. A light stroke caused his fingers to relax. He curled his fingers around hers, holding her loosely while reveling in the contact.

"If this is what you want, it's okay," she whispered.

He wanted it so bad he ached. His entire body felt electrified, light and heavy at the same time. He wanted her. Right here, right now.

He dropped her hand and stepped back. "This isn't smart." His voice sounded as if he had gargled with sand.

"These things usually aren't very smart. So what? I owe you."

Appalled at her thinking that he demanded sex in

exchange for protection, he sidled around her toward the door. "I don't take those kinds of debts." He winced at how rough he'd sounded, as if he were angry or annoyed. Her soft smile made him feel foolish. His ears burned. "It's—it's not because—you're *beautiful,* Madeline." He made his escape.

The hallway squeezed him, the stairs too steep. He felt huge and clumsy and oafish.

In the kitchen he stopped, unable to remember why he was there.

He'd been an idiot to kiss her, to smell the tantalizing sweetness of her skin and hair, to discover those full lips were as soft and sensual as they looked. Where before the attraction was abstract, now it burned.

Cartons, he remembered. He needed cartons from the barn. He fetched several, found a roll of packing tape and set it at the top of the stairs. He called her before taking the stairs down two and three at a time. Now was a fine time to change the oil in his truck.

By the time the dirty oil had drained into a pan, he could think rationally. He didn't take advantage of vulnerable women. Her cooking more than made up for her room and board. The only thing they owed each other was respect.

He was wrestling the dirty oil filter off the engine when he heard an approaching car. About time Pete arrived. It was too much to ask that the FBI would find the stolen money in a luggage locker or in Cora Shay's house, but he could hope. Wiping his hands on a rag, he stepped out of the garage and squinted down the long driveway.

A fancy red Jeep trailed a rooster-tail of dust. Carson muttered a few choice words and went out to meet his neighbor.

Chapter Nine

Madeline stood before the open closet doors. *Stupid, stupid, stupid!* She railed at herself. She could not believe an offer of sex for help had come out of her mouth. Now he thought she was an idiot—or a prostitute.

She needed to assure him she didn't trade sex for favors. To assure him...what?

That the way he looked at her, making her all hot and cold and tingly, didn't irritate her or make her feel like meat on a hook. That she fantasized about how it would feel to be naked in his arms. That his voice struck her right at the base of the throat.

Kissing him had felt so right.

She got scared and blew it.

Stupid.

She examined blouses, skirts, dresses and jackets. Jill Cody favored lightweight silks and cotton-linen blends in soft, creamy pastels and vibrant jewel tones. The clothes smelled dusty with a faint perfume of rose sachet. She laid clothes on the bed.

Before the fire, Madeline had owned one really good dress—a black, silk jersey number that had cost a ridiculous amount of money but never went out of style and was virtually indestructible. She had worn it to more gallery openings and art shows than she could recall.

She modeled a ruffled cocktail dress against her chest. Of shimmery black silk, it had spaghetti straps and a layered skirt.

She frowned at her reflection. Men had started chasing her when she began wearing a bra. Before long, she had stopped feeling flattered and started realizing she was vulnerable and asking for use and abuse. Nowadays, when men showed interest, her first reaction was annoyance. The hell of it was, she loved sex. She loved being touched and fondled and kissed all over. She loved male bodies for their size and tough skin and hairy legs and muscles. Sometimes she wished she was callous enough for pointless, promiscuous sex.

She lowered the dress, letting it dangle from her hand. Her heart was hard because every single day, life reminded her how easily it could be broken.

Carson Cody was a rarity—a man with standards. Obviously she didn't measure up.

She tossed the ruffled dress on the bed.

Trying not to think about kissing Carson was like trying to ignore a smoking volcano rumbling beneath her feet. Especially since pawing through his dead wife's belongings reminded her too vividly of how she ended up in his house in the first place. Reluctantly, hoping nothing would slap Carson's face with memories, she selected some nondescript jeans and T-shirts.

Carson let her know the cartons were in the hallway. She went to the doorway in time to hear him thundering down the stairs. Cartons and a roll of tape awaited her. She called his name. The screen door slapped against the frame.

It took three large cartons to hold Jill's shoes, belts and purses. It would take that many to contain the clothes from the closet, and she hadn't even opened the bureau drawers. She folded each item before placing it neatly in a box. A car drove up to the house. It was Tony Rule. Better him than a lynch mob, but not by much.

Tony followed Carson to the porch. She opened the window a few inches.

"—FBI looking for her?" Tony asked.

"No." Carson sounded irritated. "The FBI knows where she is. I don't know where the press is getting information."

"Is she all right? All this stuff about her dad must be freaking her out. Does she know you killed him?"

"She's fine."

"Does she know where the money is? Hey, if you need help looking for it, I'm more than happy to volunteer. I even have a metal detector. Top of the line."

Carson laughed.

Footsteps on the porch. The front door opening. Carson called up the stairs, "Madeline? Are you up for company?"

She was busy, indisposed, washing her hair. Tony was one of the guys who recognized in her the needy, lonely girl who longed for someone to love her. In Tony's eyes, she was prey. She could handle him, however, and dismiss his flirtation. She didn't want to face Carson.

"Madeline?"

"Yo, Maddy!" Tony called.

Someone needed to put that tomcat in his place. "Coming."

"Hello," she said to Tony, avoiding even a glimpse

of Carson. Every instinct warned her not to look. She would melt or swoon or otherwise thoroughly humiliate herself.

Tony ran a bold eye over her body. "You're looking good."

"Would you gentlemen care for some iced tea?" She walked past them to the kitchen.

"Ice *queen*," Tony said sotto voce.

Go to hell, she thought. She noticed the Dumb Stuff box was sealed with tape. She had opened the cabinet for glasses when, from the corner of her eye, she saw Tony pick up the phoenix vessel.

"Don't touch that!"

He almost dropped it, but caught it before it struck the table.

She gave him a hard look. "I'm very protective of my work."

Tony set down the vessel with exaggerated care and backed away, showing his palms and smiling. "What is it?"

"Art," Carson answered. "Madeline is a famous artist."

She shot him a frown. He smiled in return. He actually winked. When she gave Carson his tea, he folded his fingers over hers and lingered.

"So, Maddy," Tony said. "How does it feel to be a wanted woman? Think the FBI is offering a reward for your capture?"

Carson gave him a look askance. "Not funny, man."

"Ah, come on, if you can't laugh at a situation, it'll break you. Seriously, how are you doing? Are you over the fire scare? Feeling all right?"

"Fine." She sliced a lemon and put it and a bowl of sugar on the table. "I don't know anything about the hijacking.'' She risked a peek at Carson. He lounged on a chair, his long legs stretched out and crossed at the ankles. He didn't act as if the crack about her owing him sex offended him. He looked more interested than before. ''I'm not sure my father stole the money.''

''Why is that?''

She waited for Carson to put a halt to the discussion. His smile was sort of goofy.

''He stole cars, burglarized businesses, scammed people. He committed property crimes. He was only violent when he was drinking.'' Except for the murders at Crossruff Creek. ''Usually.''

''What about you, big guy? Think he did it?''

Carson took a long, slow drink of tea. He licked his lips. ''Not my job to speculate.''

Tony laughed and slapped his thigh. ''What's the point of having a cop for a best friend if we can't even talk about the fun stuff?''

Insensitive jerk. He acted like this was a game. A movie where all the dead guys would pick themselves up, dust themselves off and get ready to shoot the next scene. People were dead. Lives were ruined. All Tony cared about was the entertainment value.

''I have work to do. Nice seeing you again, Tony.''

''Hey, Maddy, there's a reason I came by. I have to run down to Phoenix. Business emergency. I hate making that long, lonely drive all by myself. I thought, since you probably have a bad case of cabin fever, you might like to accompany me.''

Carson startled like a horse smelling smoke. His boot heel thumped the floor.

''I'll throw in dinner at my favorite Italian restaurant. I promise to have you home at a decent hour. Unless, of course, you'd care to stay overnight in the city?''

She waited for Carson to say something about her being in protective custody. His eyes blazed and his knuckles whitened, but he kept his mouth shut. She searched for some graceful way to refuse.

The reflex to act nice like a good girl disgusted her.

"No, thanks," she said.

"It'll be fun," he said, wheedling, turning on the charm.

"I doubt it. I don't want to go. Goodbye, Tony." She went back upstairs.

CARSON PRESSED the iced tea glass against his cheek. It was beastly hot for April. The temperature was in the high nineties and not a whisper of moisture to be found. Listening to Madeline moving around upstairs, he smiled beatifically at Tony.

The boy looked as if he'd been drop-kicked and never saw the mule that did it.

"What kind of emergency takes you to Phoenix?"

"Technical stuff." Tony stared at the doorway, eyes narrowed. "That is one cold chick."

"Sour grapes, man. Face it, not every woman in the world is falling at your feet."

"Oh, she likes me all right. She's playing hard to get." His good humor returned and he hoisted his glass in salute. "Here's to the ladies worth fighting for." He drank deeply then wiped his mouth with the back of his hand. "I'm confused. She's Indian, isn't she? That picture of Shay in the paper makes him look white."

"Her mother is Apache. Shay's as Irish as they come. His parents emigrated from Ireland before he was born. Pat and Lois were good ranchers. Couldn't ask for better people."

"So what happened to the son?"

"His parents were killed in a car crash when Shay was twelve years old. He had no relatives in this country and the only thing his Irish family cared about was the money. He turned outlaw after that."

"Madeline is no outlaw."

Carson had wearied of Tony's interest in Madeline. "I have to finish my truck. Guess you need to get on the road."

"I can take a hint." Tony rose. "I am serious about having a metal detector. Top of the line. I've got that pair of ATVs collecting cobwebs, too. I'm more than happy to help you search for the loot."

"We don't know that it's buried on the ranch."

"That's what the paper implied."

"They got some facts wrong."

"So where do you think it is?"

"No idea," Carson said honestly. He couldn't stay mad at Tony. He was like an overeager hound-dog pup. No matter how often he was chastised, he rebounded, eager for more. The man didn't have a hard feeling in him. Any woman who finally managed to hog-tie Tony would have her hands full. "You can help, if you would."

"Anything for you."

"I put up signs to keep folks out. If you spot any activity over there, could you give me a holler? It might take a few hours sitting in a cell for some people to realize I mean business."

"I can do that." He turned for the back door then stopped and snapped his fingers. "I just thought of something. I've got thousands of dollars in computer equipment over at my house. I'm connected to every database and search engine in existence. You are more than welcome to use whatever you need. I won't even bill the usage fees.''

"I'll keep it in mind.''

"I mean it. I can get hold of banking records, phone logs, credit card purchases. You name it, I can dig it up.''

"Is that legal?''

Tony widened his eyes in a too-innocent look. "I swear, when I stumble across something I shouldn't, I shut my eyes.''

"Get out of my house, you clown.''

After Tony left, Carson considered climbing the stairs. If he did he would kiss her again. He wavered, frustrated with his inability to figure out what to do about Madeline.

At least he didn't have to worry about her and Tony Rule. Good enough for now.

Sergeant Pete Morales showed up an hour later. Carson asked Madeline to join them in the kitchen. She signed the authorization to exhume her father's body. She acted shy around Pete and wouldn't look him in the face. He wanted to tell her Pete was one of the good guys.

Carson explained about the letters and personal effects Madeline had received from her father, and the favor Shay wanted her to do for Deke Fry. He showed Pete the key and the passage in a letter telling Madeline about the bus station locker.

"Do you need to give the whole box to the FBI?'' Madeline asked. "I know they need the letters, but he gave me the other stuff when I was a kid.''

"Be a shame if they missed anything,'' Pete said. "Sometimes all it takes is a bit of trace evidence to break a case. They'll be careful. You'll get your things back.''

"Every little bit counts," Carson said.

"It's junk anyway," she said. A lie she wished she could believe.

Pete held up the locker key. "I talked to the FBI agent and know what he told me? Hold on to your hats. According to the manifest, that load of money weighed almost two tons."

Madeline laughed and immediately covered her mouth. "Sorry, but…two *tons?* What was it, all in nickels?"

Carson found it hard to get his mind around it, too.

Pete shrugged. "I believe it. I did some moonlighting in a casino. A money sack with a couple thousand bucks in it is heavy." He tossed the key and caught it in an overhand swipe. "Doubt it's stuffed into a locker."

"Let's hope it points to the money."

"Two tons of money," Madeline said, as if she were trying to envision what that meant. "No way my father could have dug a hole big enough to hide it all. It's crazy. Those hills are solid rock."

A SOLUTION DIDN'T OCCUR to Carson until the following day at the police station. It was getting close to lunchtime and he worried too much about Madeline to be able to concentrate on putting together the work schedule. His big worry was the press. Reporters and news vans swarmed over Ruff like magpies picking over roadkill. He'd been chasing news crews out of the station all morning.

He called Mutual Security and Assurance in Las Vegas, punched in the extension for Ivan Bannerman and reached voice mail. "This is Chief Cody, Mr. Bannerman. I need to speak to you. Call me at the station, I'll have them transfer the call to wherever I am.''

He glowered at the big map on the wall and remembered the mine. Way back when Pat Shay had bought the ranch for a song because the mine went bust. The Crossruff Mine, named for the card game the miners loved to play, was a local legend. Kids still spooked each other with sordid stories about murder and lost fortunes in gold. Pat Shay dynamited the mine entrance to keep out kids and cattle.

As kids, he and Maurice Harrigan had gone prospecting. They found the mine entrance. Maurice had wriggled his head and shoulders inside, but smelled snakes and refused to go farther.

Carson told Wanda, ''I'm out for lunch. I may be a while. Errands to run.''

''What about them?'' She pointed to the bank of windows facing Main Street where reporters wandered in search of a story.

''Same as before,'' he said loudly enough for every person in the station to hear. ''This office has no comment.''

He managed to duck out the back of the station and make it to the cruiser before reporters spotted him. The easy way would be to search for the mine's location in public records. The clerk recorder was Dee Harrigan, sister-in-law to Maurice Harrigan, and the only way to get old maps was through her.

He found it once. He'd find it again.

''WHAT IF WE FIND IT?'' Madeline asked Carson. An old mine made perfect sense.

"We'll contact the FBI. Find a pair of boots. I'll grab some water bottles and a shovel."

She didn't speak on the drive down the mesa. She pushed strands of hair off her face and wished she had asked for a hat. Heat shimmers distorted the air. Carson parked near the charred ruins of the house and van. Yellow crime-scene tape fluttered from trees. Circles of fluorescent-orange marking paint dotted the gravel. The stink tightened her scalp and chest.

"Maybe this isn't a good idea," he said.

She pulled back her shoulders. "The sooner the money is recovered, the sooner this whole mess is over with." She looked him in the eyes. "You know what? We ought to destroy the money. Like an exorcism, a cleansing."

"Will that solve anything?"

He finger-combed hair from her cheek. She caught her breath, knowing better than to read anything into the gesture, knowing she should not enjoy his touch as much as she did.

"Is it possible anything my father did can ever be made right?"

With the engine off and the air conditioner no longer blowing, the temperature soared inside the cruiser. Carson didn't seem in any hurry.

"I don't know how to answer. Only reason I agreed to help Bannerman in the first place was because I thought it might lead to others involved in the hijacking." He left the car. "Let's find that mine."

Carson settled the white Stetson on his head and led the way north away from the house. He carried a shovel. Madeline toted a long stick for poking under brush and around rocks for snakes. The ranch consisted of rocky hills, sheer rock ridges, dusty clutches of juniper and piñon, gullies like slashes cut by an impatient hand and hard-packed dirt. It was beautiful in a raw, savage sort of way, but it wasn't much fun to explore. The borrowed boots hurt her toes and ankles. Sweat pooled in the small of her back and between her breasts.

Carson pointed across an arroyo. "I think the mine is over there."

She protested with a groan. "No way my father toted two tons of money across that canyon."

"It's barely a ditch." He climbed down the brittle side. A miniature landslide of broken sandstone and gravel followed him.

Madeline searched the horizon to judge whether any of the clouds hanging low over the mesas and mountains were producing rain. Flash floods could begin miles away, without a single raindrop falling on the affected area.

Carson urged her to come on down. She followed his path. Her boots slipped and she threw herself backward to stop a fall. He caught her waist and took her weight.

He went rigid, his head cocked. "Do you hear a car?"

Sounds traveled funny in the high desert air. All she heard were squabbling crows.

The far side of the arroyo was too steep to climb. They hiked over tumbled rocks and deep, soft sand before finding a place to climb out. Carson used his hands and feet to scramble up the rocks. She handed up the shovel and snake stick.

Madeline climbed. He grabbed her arm and hauled her over the edge.

He teased, "You climb pretty good for a girl."

It didn't seem possible to like this man as much as she did. Forget their connection because of her father.

He was a cop, a well-respected member of his community, and a homeowner. She was an artist who lived from hand to mouth, with a family history straight out of a Charles Dickens novel, with only dreams to sustain her. They had nothing in common.

And yet, his smile spoke to her soul. His touch electrified her. In his house she felt safe. In his arms she felt alive.

"I really wish you would kiss me." She didn't realize she'd spoken her desire aloud until he kissed her. He tasted of salt and unbearable sweetness. She slid her hands over his biceps, along the powerful lines of his shoulders and to his neck. He dropped the tools. He slid a hand from her shoulder, down the jut of her shoulder blade and slowly along her spine, vertebra by vertebra until his hand rested softly but surely in the curve at the small of her back.

She explored the smooth ivory of his teeth. Their bodies molded breast to chest, belly to belly, thigh to thigh. His broad-brimmed hat shaded their faces from the knowing sun. Nothing else existed—not the past, not the future—there was only his mouth, the erotic eagerness of his tongue, the way his fingers flexed against her back and curled into her hair at the base of her skull. She traced his ears and stretched her thumbs along his jaw.

"Hello!"

Carson shoved Madeline behind him and drew his pistol before she gathered her wits enough to know they were not alone. She looked around wildly.

Across the arroyo, a man froze in midwave, his smile cast in stone and his eyes so wide they looked white. "Uh," he said, "don't shoot?"

Covering her mouth with her hand, Judy Green stood next to the stranger.

Madeline wasn't sure if the woman was shocked by Carson's gun or because she had caught them kissing.

Chapter Ten

Carson sized up the stranger. A tall, lanky man with ropy muscles, wearing a vest with bulging pockets and holding a camera with several film canisters affixed to the dangling strap. A reporter. Carson considered letting the man put his hands down, decided against it and turned his attention to Judy.

"I warned you, Judy Green. To top it off, you ignored the official signs I posted. I'm arresting trespassers."

Judy shrank. She knew good and well she'd blown it. Carson mused that an arrest would put her big, fat mouth to good use for once. Everybody in town would know Carson meant business.

Hands atop his head, the reporter swiveled his torso to look between Judy and Carson. "It's my fault, Chief Cody. I insisted on seeing the Shay ranch."

"You didn't see the signs?"

"We saw the cruiser. I thought it would be okay. Nick really needs to talk to you, Carson." Judy glared at Madeline. "Seeing how you're still on duty, I figured you'd be here alone."

Carson refrained from calling her a liar.

"This is all my doing, sir," the reporter said. He

spoke like a man who'd been in plenty of pickles. "I met Miss Green at the motel. Since she's a close, personal friend of yours, I asked her to get me an interview."

"Interview?"

"Nick Iola, National News Service. I have credentials." He lowered a hand toward a pocket and Carson raised the pistol. "She called the station, found out you'd gone to lunch and we looked for you. Since you weren't in town, Judy offered to take me to your place."

Judy looked ready to bolt.

"I wanted to see the fire damage and saw your squad car. All my fault. Miss Green is only along for the ride."

"Is that so? Just a friendly visit up to my place?"

"I didn't tell!" Judy shouted.

"If you're hoping to get off on a technicality, forget it. Telling and *accidentally* showing are the same thing." He wondered how long he could lock her up for trespassing.

Madeline made a disgruntled noise. She clamped her arms over her midsection, giving a glare as good as she got from Judy.

"Chief Cody, it isn't my intent to make trouble. The Worldwide hijacking is my story. I follow leads where I find them. I insisted on seeing the ranch. As I said, Miss Green is an innocent party."

Judy's eyes were too big and her chin quivered. "Nick here is a celebrity. His stories go to all the big newspapers. TV and radio, too. Ruff is gonna be famous."

Carson loosed a heavy breath. Judy made his head hurt. Madeline touched his back. She indicated wanting a private word. They walked a few yards from the arroyo. Carson kept an eye on the reporter.

Madeline whispered, "He will hurt you."

"Don't worry about me."

"How do I do that? You're taking an incredible risk letting me stay in your house. I know how people are. Quick to blame. Always ready to think the worst. You'll lose your job because of me. And what happens when your friends and neighbors find out you're harboring Frank Shay's girl? Have you even thought about this?"

Guilt pinched him. He was supposed to be the protector. He didn't mean to worry her. "I can handle those two."

"Maybe Judy isn't your girlfriend, but she sure wants to be. She feels betrayed. You can throw her into prison for twenty years and she'll still find a way to get even."

"I never touched her."

"It doesn't matter," she said through clenched teeth. "You have two choices. Either throw me out of your house or find a way to get on Judy's good side. And that reporter, too, because he's not going away."

"Or choice three." He noticed the reporter and Judy whispering together. He whipped his head about and they clamped their mouths shut. "I arrest them and let them sit in jail until I'm good and ready to let them out."

She shot him a look that gave him a start of recognition. He'd seen it often enough on Jill's face. He'd learned the hard way that it meant he was acting like an idiot, and if he wanted to redeem himself he better do exactly as she said.

"They broke the law."

Her eyebrows raised. Her lips pursed.

"What do you want me to do?"

"Give him an interview. Tell him the truth. I've got nothing to hide. He'll see how important it is nobody knows I'm here. Even Judy has to understand."

"She's a woman scorned, remember?"

Madeline fluttered her eyelashes. "More flies with honey…"

She had a point. He recognized Nick Iola's name from the newspaper stories. A face-to-face interview could clear up factual errors.

Carson requested the reporter remove the vest and toss it across the arroyo. Nick's willingness confirmed he was accustomed to working with unfriendly authorities.

Carson looked for weapons and found notebooks, pens, pencils, a cell phone, canisters of film, candy bars and other journalistic provisions. He studied the reporter's credentials. Everything looked legit.

"All right, come on over. You, too, Judy."

Judy drew back and clutched her hands to her chest. "You aren't going to put handcuffs on me, are you?"

This was a bad idea, but the best they could do. "No. Come on over."

When Nick used a prickly little bush as a handhold, it uprooted and he slid to the bottom. He scraped his knees and shins. He brushed off the dirt before helping Judy climb down.

"This is a mistake," Carson murmured.

"We can make it work to our advantage."

It had to work. Otherwise he had to send Madeline away.

Nick Iola popped over the side of the cliff. His face was leathery and his hair was liberally shot through with gray. His bright, curious eyes were young. He scrubbed his right hand on his shorts before extending it to Carson.

Grunting with effort, Judy scrambled out of the arroyo. Her face was sweaty and red. She slapped dirt off her jeans. Carson noticed the daggers she flung at Madeline.

Iola picked up his vest. "If you have to ticket me, Chief Cody, go ahead. I admit my guilt."

"Did you take pictures?"

Iola placed a protective hand over the camera. "Is that against the law, too?"

Madeline stepped forward. "I'm Madeline Shay, Mr. Iola."

"I figured that." He shook hands with her. "A lot of people want to talk to you."

"Anyone with a good reason to do so knows exactly where to find her," Carson said. "No law-enforcement agency considers her a suspect. Except in the loosest meaning of the word, she's not even a witness."

"I heard—"

"You heard wrong, sir."

"I've been covering the crime beat a long time, Chief Cody. I'm more than happy to correct errors." He wiped sweat off his forehead, leaving a streak of dirt. "The Worldwide Parcel hijacking is my story. I was first reporter on the scene in Utah. Nothing will stop me from following it through to the end."

Madeline pantomimed digging for buried money. *Tell him what we're doing,* she mouthed.

He didn't want to, but saw her point. The more open they were, the less room Iola had to speculate. "Let's walk and talk. We're looking for the Crossruff Mine."

"That's just a story," Judy said.

"It's real." He remembered it was on the side of a

hill. He walked in the direction he believed it might be. "Only thing it ever produced was heartbreak, but it's definitely real. Pat Shay blew up the entrance to keep kids from falling in."

Iola caught up to Carson. "Why are you looking for a mine?"

"Shay had a week between the time he was arrested and when he got locked up. Plenty of time to stash the money—if he had it, that is. An old mine would be perfect. Keep the stash out of the weather. Casual hikers wouldn't notice it. Nobody around to see what he's doing."

"Do you have good reason to think Shay got away with the entire shipment?"

"Nobody is positive Shay was even involved in the hijacking."

"But what do you think?"

"What I think doesn't matter. If I find a pile of money, I'll know for sure. Until then, it's anybody's guess."

"What about you, Miss Shay?"

"I didn't speak to my father." Madeline was in full Apache mode, stoic and inscrutable.

"Chief Cody, am I mistaken, or didn't a query go out from your office to the tribal police on Fort Apache regarding ten thousand dollars donated anonymously to a school? A cash donation made shortly after the hijacking. Madeline, you live on the reservation."

"There's no way to trace the source," Carson said.

"But you queried."

Madeline stopped walking. She shoved her hands into her back pockets. He read hurt as clearly as if she'd written the word on her chest in big red letters.

"I hoped the school kept the box the money came in. No such luck."

Madeline drew her head aside, and her eyes narrowed. Carson reached the top of a hill and stopped to wait for her to catch up, uncertain if she'd try. She pulled her hands from her pockets and resumed walking.

"My father sent the money," she said. "He said he won the lottery. I didn't want it so I gave it to the school."

"If you didn't talk, why give you money? Why leave you everything in his will?" Nick asked.

"I haven't the foggiest idea why he did anything. I suspect the will had to do with making sure my mother didn't benefit from his death."

At the top of the hill, she gave Carson a considering look he didn't understand, but a hunch said it wasn't kindly. "I inherited this pile of rocks and a whole lot of ill will when he died. I tried to sell the ranch. Can't find a buyer. The only reason I'm here is to get ready for a show." She smiled ruefully and scraped her boot against the dirt. "He was as much a mystery to me as he was to anyone else."

"But you're out here in this Easy Bake Oven looking for the money," Nick said.

"I want people to stop thinking I'm his accomplice."

"What about your mother? She knew Shay had a lot of money when he died. She claims you know where he hid it."

She stilled, her head high and regal. Carson caught a gleam in the reporter's eyes, the slight flare of his nostrils and knew her calm beauty affected the man. A tight fist squeezed his diaphragm.

"If Mama believed that, she'd be digging up the countryside. If she were manic, she'd level these hills."

"Manic?"

"Bipolar. Mama is mentally ill."

A grin captured the reporter's face. He pulled at his chin. "Grain of salt, got it." He turned his attention back to Carson. "So how did you make the connection between Shay and the hijacking?"

Carson searched the landscape, seeking rocks a different color than their surroundings. He told Iola about Bannerman and the anonymous tipster.

"What about the arson? Is it connected to the hijacking?"

"Only because the fire revealed Deke Fry's remains. The crimes are unrelated."

"Do you have any suspects in the arson?"

The Harrigan name showing up in the newspaper was asking for real trouble. "No."

"Oh come on, Carson," Judy said. "Everybody knows Matt and Sug did it. Only reason you don't arrest them is 'cause their daddy's a lawyer and their uncle's the mayor."

"I don't muddy names on a hunch." He took Judy aside and, for her ears only, said, "The only reason you aren't under arrest is because Madeline doesn't want to press charges. You keep running your mouth and I won't care what she wants."

Judy's lower lip pooched and she fiddled with the ends of her long, blond ponytail. She acted more like a teenager instead of a woman in her twenties. "It's the truth."

"It's not the truth until evidence proves it. Until then it's slander."

"You sure turned mean. Before she showed up you were a nice guy."

"I was nice guy until someone tried to murder her. Do you understand what that means? You are not a stupid woman. So wake up and get with the program."

She pouted like a six-year-old. "I never heard about murder."

"That's what it is. So keep your mouth closed or go back to town."

She huffed a petulant sigh, lifted her chin and stalked after Iola.

"No vinegar. Honey," Madeline whispered to him. He waved off her concerns and hiked up another hill.

THE SUN PERCHED on the mountains, turning the air deep, rich gold and the shadows long and purple. Insects revved up for an evening symphony. Madeline saw two rattlesnakes on their hike and somewhere nearby a skunk trailed noxious fumes. She was tired, hungry and anxious about being away from her beads. An hour ago Judy had complained her feet hurt and went back to the car. They didn't find anything that resembled a mine shaft.

Madeline warmed to the reporter. Nick Iola had a sense of humor. He enjoyed talking, so it wasn't long before she learned he lived in Las Vegas, had been married and divorced three times, worked as a war correspondent, been short-listed twice for a Pulitzer, been fired from two major newspapers and he owned three cats. He appeared oblivious to the heat and the rough hike.

With night approaching, they headed back to the ruined house. Unhappy about having to face Judy again, Madeline dawdled. Judy probably cared a whole lot less about Madeline being Frank Shay's daughter and a whole lot more about Madeline kissing the man Judy wanted.

They followed a deer path, walking single file through the brush. The biting flies disappeared, but mosquitoes whined forward to take their place. Bats cast flitting shadows overhead.

"So," Nick asked, "what do you think about there being a hijacker on the loose and unaccounted for?"

Carson ducked beneath a low branch. "All I can say is Bannerman's information pans out so far."

They were close enough to the house to smell the charred wood and ashes. Madeline preferred the smell of skunk. She'd never smell wood smoke again without a twinge of unease.

Nick looked over his shoulder at Madeline. "Did anyone other than the cops ever talk to you about your father? Claiming to be an old friend or something?"

She slapped at mosquitoes. "Only collection agencies."

Both Carson and Nick turned around. She pulled back. "What?"

"Was this one agency or several? Do you remember the names?"

Wishing she had kept her mouth shut, she shrugged and showed her palms. "I don't know. Two years ago? I only remember because a guy got nasty with me. He said he would sue me for the debt. Mama finally told him my father was in prison."

"Did the calls stop?"

"I think so."

"Did he ask about assets?" Nick asked. "Bank accounts or real estate?"

"He didn't ask me."

The path ended abruptly at the edge of the clearing. A dusty, rusted Volvo station wagon was parked behind the police cruiser.

Carson planted his hands on his hips. He stared at the Volvo. "Judy? Judy!"

"Hey!" came an answering cry from the end of the driveway. Judy ran toward them, her ponytail bouncing. "Carson! There's somebody up at your house. I saw lights." She skidded to a stop and bent over, grasping her thighs and panting from the run. "You *never* leave the lights on."

Carson and Madeline searched the mesa, even though trees blocked the view. "The sun is hitting the windows," Carson said.

Judy insisted. "I heard a car. I saw the lights come on." She shot Madeline a snotty look. "You got yourself another woman up there?"

He caught Madeline's hand, practically dragging her to the car. By the time she had her seat belt fastened, he was wheeling the cruiser in a circle.

"It could be Sergeant Morales," she said helpfully.

"Or someone giving my house the same treatment they gave yours." Gravel crunched beneath the tires. He slowed enough to make certain there wasn't any traffic on the road before gunning the engine. Madeline grabbed the armrest, clinging to it for dear life. Carson leaned over the steering wheel to peer up at the mesa. "Do you see anything?"

"I am so sorry. I'm causing you nothing but trouble. I'll get out of here. I promise. I'll—"

"Madeline," he interrupted. "Hush. You're anything but trouble to me."

At his driveway, he stopped to stare at the road. A light haze of dust hovered. Not a breath of wind disturbed it and it looked like fog in the headlights. Carson headed for the house.

The Volvo's headlights bounced crazily as Nick tried to keep up on the unfamiliar road.

The house was dark. Tony Rule's Jeep was parked at the base of the porch steps.

"I'm going to punch him in the nose." Carson parked behind the Jeep.

Tony rose from his seat on the porch step. He waved.

Carson stormed out of the cruiser. "What were you doing in my house?"

Tony backed a step. "Whoa, you're really mad. What's the matter?"

"What's the matter is that I don't like people snooping around in my house. Not even you, Tony."

Tony lowered his head. Iola arrived. He and Judy stuck close to the Volvo.

"I wasn't in your house, man. I figured you'd be home from work. I brought some bread and cheese from a gourmet shop in Phoenix." He touched his foot to a brown paper bag with a string handle.

Carson turned to Judy. "You swore there were lights inside the house."

"Uh, well, uh, guess it was headlights." She smiled wanly. "Hi, Tony. Sorry."

Carson was a real bear when riled. Madeline felt bad for Tony and almost felt bad for Judy.

"Can we discuss this inside?" Madeline asked Carson. "I'm dying for a cold drink."

Unlocking the door, Carson said, "I'm sorry. I'm a tad jumpy these days."

"No problem." Tony didn't sound convinced. "Can't be too careful, even with your best buddy, right?"

Carson asked Madeline to serve drinks in the kitchen while he made some phone calls.

Judy hooked her arm with Tony's while she apologized profusely for her mistaken observation. They walked down the hall together. Nick gave Carson a considering look before he followed the pair. Madeline hung back.

She whispered, "You cannot believe Tony actually broke into the house, can you?"

"I don't know."

"He's your friend. You trust him."

"Yeah, yeah, good old best buddy."

Now he was being churlish, angry for letting Judy get him worked up, and embarrassed about being wrong.

"How about I fix sandwiches. You must be hungry."

He picked up the telephone. "I'll be there in a minute."

In the kitchen Judy poked through a bowl of beads. Without a word, Madeline took the bowl and cleared her work off the table. Judy turned her attention to Tony, saying she hadn't seen him around lately and how was he doing and had he bought any new cars since she talked to him last.

A perfect match, Madeline thought while she pulled leftover roast pork and baked chicken from the refrigerator. Within minutes Nick fell under Tony's spell, sounding delighted to answer all of Tony's questions about the hijacking. Madeline tuned them out, envisioning patterns and stitching techniques while she washed lettuce and sliced tomatoes.

Carson entered the kitchen. Still in uniform, he'd removed his hat, utility belt and holster. Tony placed the paper sack, dolled up with a fancy logo, onto the table. He produced a six-pack of beer.

Everyone accepted a beer except Madeline. She declined, politely.

"Indians can't handle liquor," Judy said.

Madeline bristled.

"They're all drunks on the reservation. It's a crying shame. All that poverty and disease. It's like a third-world country."

Madeline refused to argue with that woman about life on the reservation. Yes, there was poverty and disease, but there were also artists and ranchers and builders and teachers. Living on the rez didn't condemn anyone to a third-world lifestyle, any more than living in a city meant living in a ghetto.

Judy stood. "Guess I can set the table. I know where everything is." She peered over Madeline's shoulder. "Sandwiches, hmm? Men need a hot meal in the evening." She opened the freezer compartment, looked inside, and sighed. "Looks like you gobbled down all my casseroles, Carson. Too bad. I could have put together a decent meal for you."

Madeline sensed Carson's discomfort, but this was his house. It wasn't her place to put Judy in her place.

Tony offered Madeline loaves of bakery bread. "I love sandwiches. Know how to do a Dagwood?"

Judy shot her a withering look and Madeline wanted to say, *Oh, give me a break!* but she managed to hold it in. She unwrapped the bread and lost herself in the rich, yeasty aroma.

"Tell me more, Nick," Tony said. "Old Carson here is so closemouthed I'm surprised he doesn't eat through a straw. This hijacking sounds like the crime of the century. You thinking about writing a book?"

"I've considered it," Nick said.

"None of the money was ever recovered?"

"Not a dime." It took very little urging for Nick to regale Tony with detailed descriptions of the downed airplane and murder victims.

Madeline carried a platter of sandwiches to the table. It was set for four.

Judy tsked. "Too bad we couldn't have my tuna casserole for supper. There were never any leftovers 'cause Carson couldn't get enough. I took care of Carson for nearly a year, Nick. Poor guy was living on canned fruit and canned spaghetti before I stepped in. Now it's back to cold sandwiches. Oh, well."

Madeline put another place setting on the table.

"Where I come from," Judy said, "hired help don't eat at the table."

"Not enough room at the card table in the old trailer, huh?" Madeline said.

Carson snorted, then coughed and set his beer bottle hard on the table. Nick looked interested, but confused. Tony roared with laughter.

Judy's face blazed crimson. "That's real funny. An Indian calling me trailer trash."

"Do you prefer hillbilly? Redneck?"

"At least I ain't demon seed. Nobody in my family ever went around butchering innocent folks. You got some nerve running around this house like you own the place. It's sick. Just plain sick! Carson should gun you down just like he did your old man."

All traces of humor gone, Carson rose. His face darkened and his eyes were bleak. "Madeline is my guest."

"She's your *whore*. How can you stand to touch her? It gives me the creeps just thinking about it."

Madeline's hands itched with the urge to jump on the

blonde, to slap and choke and make her cease the ugliness.

"Uh," Nick muttered. He set his beer bottle very gently on the table. "I just remembered I'm expecting a very important phone call back at the hotel."

"Me, too," Judy said inanely. "The thought of sitting at a table with that whore makes me want to puke."

"Get out of my house," Carson said. "You are never welcome here again."

"Maurice is right. You cracked up. Lost all your marbles." Judy sneered at Madeline. "Guess you're the straw that broke him. Hope you're happy." She sniffed, did an about-face and stomped away.

"I apologize," Nick said, looking between Carson and Madeline. "I—didn't—I wasn't aware—"

"Not your fault," Carson said. "I'll see you out."

Madeline covered her face with a hand. She should not have let the blonde get to her. As soon as Judy hit town, she'd be yelling from the rooftops.

"I get it," Tony said. "Little Judy has the hots for Carson. I wonder how I missed that."

Madeline listened while Carson escorted Judy and the reporter outside. "I bet she runs straight to the mayor."

Tony chuckled. "So? You'll get arrested for stealing her man?"

She gave him a hard look. "The mayor happens to be the father of the boy my father killed."

Tony winced and slapped his forehead. "Oh, yeah, I know that. I didn't live here when it happened. I guess he won't be too happy about his police chief putting you up."

"I couldn't stand it if Carson lost his job because of me."

He waved a hand like a model pointing out a game-show prize. ''The offer stands. I'll be more than happy to put you up in my place.'' He winked. ''I do have a spare bedroom. It even has a lock on the door.''

''Inside or outside?'' Madeline asked.

He scrunched his face. ''Ouch. The lady has teeth.''

Carson returned. ''I should have fired that woman a long time ago. Tuna casserole.'' He made a face. ''Turns my stomach thinking about it. Sorry about that, Madeline.''

''What did you say to her?''

''I should have arrested her when I had the chance. Damn it, bad enough I have to worry about the reporter. He'll probably keep his mouth shut so he can use me as a source later, but Judy? I don't know if she can keep quiet.''

''So what were you guys doing? How did you hook up with Judy and the reporter?'' Tony helped himself to sandwiches. Madeline handed him the lettuce and tomatoes.

''We were down at Madeline's place. Judy was showing Nick around and he wanted to see the burn site.''

''Bet you were looking for the loot, weren't you?''

After Judy, Tony was a model of tact and diplomacy. Madeline couldn't rouse enough energy to feel annoyed. ''It's too much money to hide. Even if he knew about the mine, how could he move all that rock?''

Carson piled sandwiches on his plate. ''I know for a fact there's enough of a hole for a boy to wiggle into. The rocks are loose. A man could clear the entrance by hand then put the rocks back.''

''What's with the mine?'' Tony asked.

Carson told him the mine's history and how he'd seen it when he was a boy. He ate a big bite of sandwich, swallowed a gulp of beer, and said, "Trouble is, I've forgotten completely where it is."

"Maybe Shay left a treasure map," Tony said hopefully.

Carson shared a weary look with Madeline. "The way things are going, I doubt we'll get that lucky."

Chapter Eleven

Madeline washed dishes. After Tony's departure, the house seemed too quiet and big. It didn't feel safe. She scrubbed the table, putting muscle into the task, wishing she could wipe away Judy's venom. Carson came inside, carrying the scent of hay and horse. She moved aside so he could wash his hands in the empty side of the double sink.

Stupid, *stupid* man, she thought. He might as well be wearing blinders. He refused to see what he did to himself. He refused to consider another way.

He shook his wet hands and she handed him a towel.

"Don't pay Judy any mind." His voice was raw with apology. "She's ignorant."

His kindness undid her. Her eyes filled with grit.

"I don't belong here and you know it. You think you're doing the right thing. What good will that do when Ruff turns its back on you? When your friends go cold? When you lose your job? I'm not worth it."

He tried to take her hand, but she danced out of reach.

"Judy's right. All I do is hurt you."

Arms crossed, he cocked a hip and leaned against the counter. His unflinching perusal shook her and she wanted to push him out of the way, but if she touched him, she'd melt.

"I never imagined you had so much self-pity," Carson said.

Hurt underscored the comment. Better he hurt a little bit now than suffer worse later. "You're the one full of self-pity. That's the only reason you want me here. You think you deserve the pain."

"And what about you?" he snapped.

"What about me?"

He nodded grimly, his cheek muscles tight. "I killed your father. Don't tell me you don't think about *that* when you look at me."

"As a matter of fact, I don't."

"Liar."

She wanted to throw something at him. "At least I don't live in a mausoleum. This house is a shrine to your wife. Since I've been here, you haven't gotten one friendly phone call. It's all business or cranks. You've lived here all your life, but Tony is your only friend? Are you scared someone will slip up and say something about Jill?"

His eyes were ice. "I don't know what you're talking about."

She threw a towel. It smacked his chest and fell to the floor. "You most certainly do! Jill! Jill Jill Jill Jill! It makes you sick to hear her name in my mouth and that's what you really want from me!"

"You've no idea what I really want from you. Since you're in a state and unfit for company, I'm going to watch some television."

"Thick," she muttered, and scrubbed out the sink. She turned her energy on the stove and the top of the refrigerator and the floor. No amount of sweat erased

Judy's nasty voice from her mind. Nothing changed the truth. She had to get out of here.

"WANDA," Carson said, "bring me yesterday's activity report."

Yesterday's argument with Madeline gnawed at him. She hadn't spoken a single word to him while fixing breakfast this morning. He wanted to apologize, but he wasn't certain exactly where her anger had come from, or why she directed it at him. She had no cause to feel guilty about her father's crimes.

The dispatcher puffed up like an offended chicken. "If anything important had happened, I'd have called your cell."

"I'm not accusing you of dereliction of duty. While you're at it, bring me the maintenance logs for the vehicles and the latest equipment survey." Ignoring her confusion, he entered his office. He felt restless, antsy. The rumor mill wasn't churning this morning about Madeline, meaning Nick Iola and Judy Green were keeping their promises to stay quiet.

Carson's real worry was that Madeline might leave. She'd end up like old Luke, living in a shack constructed of scraps and cardboard, tolerated only because it brought so many people the satisfaction of looking down their noses at him.

She was too proud to accept money from him. The one time he had broached the subject, she about snapped his head off. Her bead art was valuable. He could buy a piece for enough money to lease a small apartment. And then what? She had no transportation, no household goods.

Rage climbed through his chest and tightened his scalp. If she were anyone else, the people of Ruff would fall all over themselves to help. They'd give her clothes, pots and pans, food, money and some good old boy would have put a new battery in an old car and told her to use it as long as she wanted.

They put Madeline in the same box as her father, and refused to see her as completely separate.

It made him ashamed of his town, ashamed of the people he considered friends. He was ashamed of their close-mindedness and bigotry.

Wanda arrived with the stack of paperwork. She plopped it in front of him. "I've been taking care of this. You haven't showed a lick of interest in…a long time."

"Do you mean since Jill died? You're right and I apologize for dumping my paperwork in your lap. I appreciate you helping out in my time of grief. It's high time I get back to pulling my weight around here."

She stared at him as if he had sprouted a second head. "Well, okay then. It is about time." She executed an about-face and marched out of the office.

He was in the middle of juggling the budget to pay for new tires when Wanda announced the FBI had arrived. She looked ready to wriggle right out of her skin. She had worked for the Ruff police department for over thirty years and this was the first time a real live FBI agent had graced the station. She begged with her eyes for Carson to keep his office door open so she could eavesdrop. He almost hated to disappoint her.

In suit and tie, looking more like an accountant than a law-enforcement official, the FBI agent lugged a large box into Carson's office. He set it on the floor.

"You must be Agent Lipton," Carson said, shaking hands with the man. "Nice to put a face to the voice on the phone."

"We appreciate your department's cooperation, Chief Cody. You've been a big help."

"Glad to hear it." He tried not to look like an eager kid, but the box intrigued him. "Have a seat. What can I do for you?"

"This is actually a courtesy call." He nodded at the box. "And a delivery for Miss Shay. Hard as it to believe, the locker was untouched for four years. It got overlooked. Good thing. It's given us our first real break."

"What's in the box?"

Agent Lipton chuckled. "Arts-and-crafts supplies. Shay left a note for his daughter. I brought a copy." He pulled a folded sheet of paper from his inside pocket and handed it over the desk.

Carson read aloud.

"Happy Birthday, baby. I'm out of time to pack up your present and mail it. By the time you get this I will be in prison. I'm not fighting the charges. I'm pleading guilty, baby, just for you, to prove I'm going straight. My life of crime is officially over. So you forgive your old man. I'll be out in two years, three at most. Then we start over, you and me. With my lottery winnings we will have the kind of life most folks only dream about. I will write you every day. You make lots of pretty things. I want to see it all. I am so proud of you. Write me. I love you.

Daddy.

PS, if a man by the name of Jonas Wit ever contacts you, you don't know where I am, okay? He thinks I owe him money, but I don't."

"Going straight, huh? Any idea who Jonas Wit is?"

"We'll figure it out. In the meantime, Mr. Going-Straight tucked a packet of hundreds in the locker for Miss Shay. Five thousand dollars and he forgot to remove the casino wrapper. Step one in the money trail."

"I'll be damned. What about DNA results?"

"Not in yet. My boss wants to hold off searching Miss Shay's property until we get solid proof placing Shay on the Worldwide plane. I have a hunch we'll find what we're looking for."

"If the DNA doesn't match, what then?"

Lipton stroked his chin. "My boss is conservative, but not even he can let the opportunity pass. Now I wonder if you would escort me to Miss Shay. I'd like to give her the box. I also have the personal items she provided with the letters."

"It's not evidence?" He pointed his chin at the box. "Isn't that considered stolen goods?"

Lipton cleared his throat. "Our forensic team went over everything. We kept the letters and, of course, the cash. I made an executive decision. Miss Shay has been more than cooperative with us, so I'll give her the benefit of the doubt."

"Kind of you."

"We're not all heartless bureaucrats." He flashed a smile. "Contrary to Mrs. Cora Shay's opinion. Have you ever met her?"

"Haven't had the pleasure."

"Keep denying yourself. We presented a warrant to search her home and had to have the tribal police restrain her while we searched."

"Find anything?"

"Nothing to do with Shay or the hijacking. We did

find jars full of fingernail clippings and hair trimmings. Mrs. Shay claims she keeps them so her enemies can't get her.''

The image that roused was downright ugly. ''Did she say anything about Madeline?''

Lipton blew a whistle of amazement. ''Oh, yeah, we got quite an earful. She talks like her husband and daughter are Hitler, Idi Amin and Saddam Hussein rolled into one. She accused us of being her daughter's henchmen.''

''She's mentally ill.''

''I figured that out. Crazy or not, she's got everybody down in Fort Apache convinced Miss Shay is sitting on a fortune. She's smart to stay away.''

''Would you care to ride with me, or follow in your car?'' Carson asked.

''I'll follow.'' He glanced at his watch. ''I'm due in Flagstaff this afternoon.''

Carson offered to carry the box and Lipton let him. On the way down the back stairwell, Lipton asked, ''Have you seen the insurance investigator around?''

''Can't say that I have. Reckon he got mad and went home. I've been waiting for lawyers from Mutual Security and Assurance to call me, but so far nothing. Hope it's a good sign.''

''Hmm.''

Carson didn't like the sound of that. He stopped on the second-floor landing. ''What?''

''Our field agent in Las Vegas visited Mutual Security and Assurance. According to them, Mr. Bannerman took a month-long vacation. He is on a photo safari in the Far East. Not only was Mr. Bannerman *not* investigating the Worldwide hijacking, but that the case is inactive.''

Carson snorted, indignant. ''Little squirrel is free-lancing. What do you want to bet that he worked out a deal with his so-called anonymous informant to split the finder's fee? I should have checked him out from the beginning.''

''If you can spare a man or two to find him, I'm sure I can convince him to cooperate.''

''I'll do that.'' Mentally kicking himself for sloppiness, Carson continued down the stairs.

When he reached the house, with Lipton in a sedan behind him, he took a few moments to look around and make sure all was well.

He carried the box inside and called, ''Madeline, there's a gentleman here to see you.''

Silence replied. She wasn't working on her beads in the kitchen. She wasn't upstairs. Scalp itching in apprehension, he checked her bedroom. Her boxes were still there. If she was in the barn playing with Rosie, she'd have heard the cars. He went back downstairs intending to check the barn anyway when he noticed a note on the refrigerator.

''I took Rosie out for a little exercise. I'll be back before dark. M.''

He crushed the note in his fist. He had a good idea where she'd gone and it had nothing to do with exercise.

IT WAS AN EXERCISE in futility. Try as she might, Madeline could not get inside her father's head.

She gulped water then screwed the cap onto the canteen and hung it from the saddle horn. She patted Rosie's sweaty neck. The trail along Crossruff Creek from Carson's property to hers wasn't difficult, but the mare was out of shape. Madeline loosened the reins and let Rosie take another sip of water. Rosie blew noisy bubbles in the shallow water. She hoped the horse didn't have trouble going back up the trail.

If Carson turned her out for abusing his wife's horse, she deserved it. She welcomed it. His hatred would make it easier to leave.

She sighed, wishing she could hate him for killing her father. But she hadn't hated him or blamed him when it happened. She didn't hate him now. Depending on his kindness churned her up inside. It made her self-reliance feel like the worst sort of lie.

She turned her attention to the creek. Her father had murdered Jill Cody and Billy Harrigan in the shade of the cottonwood trees. She shifted on the saddle and frowned at the junipers and piñons between this creek and where the house once stood. She smelled ashes. If Jill and Billy had talked loudly or laughed, her father would have heard them from the house. He could have approached them without fear of being seen. The murders happened in full daylight. He could not have mistaken them for law-enforcement officers.

She urged Rosie across the stream. Her unshod hooves clunked against the rocks. The creek offered little obstacle to the mare's long legs and eagerness to reach a patch of grass. Madeline dismounted and left the reins trailing. She untied a spade from the back of the saddle.

She walked along the bank. She studied the creek, the trees and rock formations. She poked the ground with the spade. The topsoil was thin and sandy, held together with tough grasses and weeds. Cottonwood saplings and willows reached like greedy fingers for the sun.

She tried to imagine what her father saw. She sat on a fallen cottonwood trunk and rested her hands on the spade handle.

So her father buried a body under the house. He's preparing to dig up thirty million dollars when he hears Jill Cody and Billy Harrigan down at the creek.

Madeline shook her head, unable to fathom why her father murdered Jill and Billy. Frank Shay had been many things in his violent life, but stupid enough to think a woman and boy were the police? Maybe he thought they were treasure hunters. Surely if he sneaked up on them and listened, he'd have heard them talking about looking for runaway goats, not hidden loot. So why not lay low until they went away? Nothing indicated that Jill or Billy got anywhere near the house. Nothing indicated Jill and Billy, or anyone in the area, had any idea Frank Shay was on the ranch.

Gooseflesh rose on her arms and she scrubbed the bumps away. Poor Carson. She couldn't imagine how he maintained his sanity after seeing his wife and a boy gunned down. Her chest ached and her eyes burned. Tears she could not shed for herself fell for Carson. Bent over, her face in her hands, she turned her emotions free, shedding guilt, grief, pain and sorrow as she sobbed and wept until she was drained, her chest and throat sore, her energy sapped. She wiped the tracks away with the back of a hand.

She turned her face to the dappled sunlight and waited until she could breathe without her chest hitching. She couldn't remember the last time she had cried like that.

She picked at the log. The wood was silver with age and pieces crumbled into dust at a touch. A lizard darted past her fingers, startling her before her brain registered it had legs and was therefore not a snake. She watched it slither into the trunk.

The hole was about a foot long and four inches wide. Madeline poked a willow switch into the hollow trunk. She considered sticking her hand inside, but where a lizard could go so could a snake.

She stepped away to better see the log in its entirety. Alive, the tree would have been a giant specimen of a high-desert cottonwood, sixty or seventy feet tall and perhaps eight feet in diameter.

She sniffed, wishing for a handkerchief. She struck the hole with the spade. Splinters and dust flew. She dug and worried the brittle outer wood and spongy interior, peeling away chunks until the hole was big enough to look inside.

Nothing except for agitated bugs.

She overturned rocks and peered inside hollow logs and shoved the spade deeply into any place in the earth that looked soft. She searched the trees for any suspicious bundles stashed in the woody forks.

"Two tons of cash," she muttered. "How in the world do you hide two tons of cash?"

In a great big hole, that was how. He'd have needed dynamite to blast a big enough hole in the bedrock.

Unless… She turned her attention on the water. Spring fed, the creek ran low in the baking heat of summer and high with snowmelt in the winter. She sat to pull off her boots. Jill's boots, she thought with a wave of pure hatred toward her father. A woman who should have lived to be a hundred, loving her good husband and being loved in return. She waded into the stream.

She had to find the money, end this madness, and get out of Carson's life.

Compared to the sun's heat, the water was icy. A thin

squeak escaped her. Smooth rocks, rough sand and
gravel, and slime made the footing treacherous. She
shoved the spade into the sandy bottom. The water
clouded with silt.

Digging a hole in a creek should be easy, but when
she scooped out a spadeful of gravel and sand, the water
pushed sand and gravel into the hole. She set the spade
on the bank and used her hands to pile rocks in a clumsy
dam. She dug again. A few inches down, the gravel
ended, leaving only slippery sand that seemed to bubble
up from the center of the world. She dug faster, sending
small rocks flying and splashing and banging against
rocks sticking out of the water. She shoved and lifted
and flung until sweat streamed into her eyes and soaked
her neck. Her shoulders ached. Other than muddy water
and a lot of noise, she had little to show for her efforts.

She did not see how it was possible for her father to
have created a hiding place under the creek. He'd have
had to dam the water then use some kind of machinery
to scoop through the wet sand, and figure out how to
waterproof the hole.

She turned for the bank. Mossy rocks were as slippery as wax. She felt her foot slip, but no amount of
arm flailing and jerking for balance stopped the fall.

Water rushed past her elbows and wicked up her
shirt. She spit dirty water out of her mouth and wiped
it from her eyes. She fished out her locket, checking to
make sure it wasn't wet. Water beaded on the alumi-
num, but it wasn't waterlogged. The end of her braid
curled like a snake, undulating downstream with the
current. Sand and silt seeped inside her clothing.

She lost the spade. She struggled from the hole and
the sucking, squishy sound made her laugh. She groped
for the spade.

Rosie nickered low and welcoming. Madeline followed the mare's line of sight.

Carson walked from the trees, sunglasses shielding his eyes. His mouth was a grim line. His hands clenched and relaxed with the rhythm of his pace. In all her splashing around she'd failed to hear him drive onto the property.

Madeline saw herself through his eyes. Soaking wet while his old horse—his wife's horse—stood in the very place where his wife was murdered.

Excuses wouldn't cut it. Nor would apologies.

"Madeline? What the hell are you doing?"

"Looking for a shovel—oh, found it." Madeline held up the dripping spade. Arms crossed, big shoulders squared, he glowered down at her. She sloshed out of the creek. Wet denim clasped her legs. Sand chafed her skin. Physical discomfort paled next to the weight of his hard perusal. She felt like a little kid caught in a prank.

"I don't appreciate you taking Rosie without permission. She isn't shod." He put a shoulder against the mare's shoulder and lifted her left front hoof.

"I kept to the trail and let her choose the pace."

He checked the mare's hooves, then slipped a hand beneath the saddle blanket. Rosie's big ears flopped and her eyelids lowered, as if his attention felt as good as a massage.

Madeline wrung water from her braid. "I wouldn't hurt Rosie. I'd never do that."

"She's blind in her right eye."

His concern went beyond the mare. The very air around him shimmered with anger.

"I didn't mean to scare you," she said. "That wasn't my intent."

"I *was* scared," he snapped. "What do I have to do? Lock you up for your own protection? Put a chain on your ankle?"

She curled her lips between her teeth. Pressure was building, and it grew difficult keeping her temper in check. "I'm sorry."

"Sorry doesn't cut it!" His voice boomed across the creek. "People want to hurt you. Do you get that? Do you understand? I'm doing my best to keep you safe, but you have to act the fool? Woman, are you stupid?"

Her spine turned to steel. "You're the stupid one! I didn't ask for your help. You know what will happen when people find out I'm in your house and you do it anyway!"

"I should let you live in a burned-up house with no food, no transportation, no clothes? You might think it's pride, sweetheart, but it's just plain idiotic in my book." He kicked a stone, sending it skittering into the creek. "This old horse has more sense than you. Chickens have more sense."

It wasn't bright to take off when there were so many hostile people in the area. On the other hand, nobody else yelled at her as if she were a naughty child.

"I deeply, sincerely apologize," she said, each word solid ice. "I will return Rosie to the barn. I won't even ride. I will walk her back up the trail." She snatched up the boots and the spade. "I will rub her down and clean her hooves and give her a handful of molasses mash. I will rub liniment into her knees and hocks. Then I will never, *ever,* for as long as I live, touch anything that belongs to you!"

Rosie turned her head because of her blind eye. She looked as if she watched a tennis match.

Madeline's wet feet collected debris. They were too

dirty to put on the boots. Refusing to look at Carson she slung the boots by their laces over the saddle horn, tied the spade behind the saddle and picked up Rosie's reins. With as much dignity as soaked, squeaking jeans allowed, she led the mare back across the creek and up the trail.

"Madeline, do not walk away from me."

Head high, with warm horse breath wafting over her arm, she kept walking. She was too mad, too upset, too heart-wounded to acknowledge what the rough, sun-baked trail did to her feet. Her ancestors had walked barefoot. She could, too.

Carson jumped the creek. Rosie balked. Madeline tugged lightly on the reins and the mare resumed walking.

"Now you're being ridiculous," Carson said.

"Stupid and ridiculous," she said. "The things a girl can learn."

The trail meandered through the scrubby piñons and skirted wind-worn sandstone formations. The dirt was hot as a pancake griddle, but Madeline kept walking.

"Will you at least tell me what you were doing?"

"Looking for the money," she flung over her shoulder. "I thought maybe he buried it under the creek. It's stupid, but what do you expect from a woman like me?"

"Stop."

"And when I find the money, I'm getting out of your hair. I don't want the finder's fee, but I'll take it for no other reason than because you are too damned pig-headed to protect yourself."

The trail narrowed. Along with the sharp rocks and stickers, she risked Rosie stomping on her feet.

"I am sick and tired of you dreaming up motives for

me.'' He was right on Rosie's heels and didn't raise his voice. ''I am thirty-nine years old and the chief of police, for God's sake. You don't think I know what I'm doing?''

''As a matter of fact, I don't think you do. Admit it, you blame yourself for Jill's death.''

''Has it ever occurred to you, just once, that maybe I care about you? That it has nothing to do with the past and everything to do with the fact that you need help and I can give it?''

She flipped her wet braid. Where the shirt was damp it cooled her, but the shoulders and collar were dry, where she needed cooling the most. Abrasions burned her inner thighs. If she believed his words for a second, she'd be lost. She walked faster.

''Damn it, Madeline! Stop!''

''If I don't? You'll shoot me?''

She had trekked twenty feet before it hit her that all she heard was the clop-clopping of Rosie's hooves.

Rigid as a child's stick-figure drawing, Carson stood on the trail. He had pulled off the sunglasses. Naked pain marked his eyes and mouth. She gasped and covered her wretched mouth with her hand.

''Oh, my God, I didn't mean that,'' she whispered.

He licked his lips. His broad chest rose and fell.

Why not just throw stones at him, she wondered in bitter disgust. Stab him in the gut. Bust his kneecaps. It couldn't hurt worse than what she had said. She dropped the reins. Rosie stretched her head longingly toward the barn. Unable to muster a shield against pain, Madeline limped down the trail.

Carson looked away. His throat worked and his lips were so tight they were pale.

Tears rose anew, as appalling as they were confusing.

She willed Carson to look at her, to forgive her. He stared into the distance.

She touched his arm. He shivered like a horse shaking a fly. "Please, I didn't mean that. Please believe me. I don't want to hurt you. I never want to hurt you. That's why I have to leave. I do care about you. I care about you more than I ever thought possible and I can't stand the idea of harming you."

"Do you know what the worst thing is about shooting your father?" he said so softly she had to hold her breath to hear him. "It was how much I wanted him dead. I didn't hesitate to draw down on him. Didn't feel a twinge about pulling the trigger. Even if he hadn't been pointing a rifle at me, even if he'd been on the ground with handcuffs on his wrists and shackles on his legs, I'd have shot him. That's what I have to look at in the mirror." He looked at her and frowned. "Why are you crying?"

She used the flats of both hands to scrub away hot tears. "I never cry." Her throat ached worse than her burning feet. "I wish I'd never come here. I wish none of this had ever happened."

"No more than me. I'm getting tired of beating myself up for all the things I should have done."

"What could you have done?" she asked.

He shrugged. "I should have been paying attention. I should have known Frank had come back." His gaze went distant. "I could have put up a better fence to keep the damned goats from wandering. I'm the one who told Jill to hire Billy to help her with the animals."

"I thought you said Jill adored Billy?"

He shrugged again and scuffed his boot in the dirt. "Well, yeah. We couldn't have kids so she sort of adopted him. I suppose he'd have helped her whether I paid him or not." He lifted a hand as if to touch her, and hesitated. "It's all useless. Nothing I do will ever change the past. I do know one thing that can change right now."

She pinched the bridge of her nose to stop a fresh rise of tears. "What's that?"

"You can stop acting like any of this is your fault. You can stop accusing me of blaming you for what you did. I don't blame you for anything. Not for him, not for the Harrigan boys burning your place or Judy Green acting like a nitwit. I'm helping you because you need help and I can give it. I care about you."

She sat on a boulder and lifted a foot onto her lap. She picked gravel from the sole. "I'm not used to having people care about me. After what Judy said, it really hit hard how impossible this situation is. Nothing will be right until I'm gone." Wincing, she plucked a thorn from her instep and rubbed the stinging spot with her thumb. "If I find the money, it's over. Case closed, I'm out of here. I will accept the reward money. Not because I want to, but because I have to."

He tucked the glasses into his shirt pocket and took a seat on a boulder across the trail from her. The creek was singing and so were the birds. Saddle leather squeaked when Rosie shifted.

"So that's what you want," he said. "To get away from me."

His flat comment broke her heart. She plucked at the damp shirt. She smelled like waterlogged weeds. "It's what I need to do."

"I don't want you to go."

She waited for the "but." The longer she waited the more she believed.

He wanted her.

She didn't know what to do with the knowledge. No one had ever wanted her before, not without some huge strings attached. The only strings involved with Carson were those that had latched into her heart, filling her with a yearning so sweet and powerful sometimes she dropped what she was doing and let the feeling rush through her. She could not ignore her feelings for him or shut them away and pretend they didn't exist. His bluntness made it impossible for her act as if he meant anything else.

Chapter Twelve

Madeline did not know how long she and Carson sat on opposite sides of the narrow trail. Long enough to realize she wanted his forgiveness and goodwill. She felt terrible about scaring him. It was strange having someone care enough to worry about her absence, but here it was.

And then to get mad and throw a tantrum like a thwarted kid. All it had gained her were torn-up feet and Carson looking as if she'd kicked him in the belly.

She crossed the trail and settled both hands on his shoulders. His eyes took her breath away. She could die happy if his eyes were the last thing she saw.

"Please accept my apology. I didn't think." She smoothed wayward hair off his forehead. "Where's your hat?"

"In the car." He settled his hands on her hips, resting them lightly.

She kissed him. A quick and tender kiss giving him no opportunity to either kiss her back or rebuff her. "Do you accept my apology?"

"I'm real mad about you taking off." His eyes softened and so did his mouth.

She kissed him again, lingering over the salty sweetness of his lips. He smelled of shaving cream. She drew back a few inches until his eyes came into focus. "Still mad?"

His fingers tightened over her hips. Shivers of pure pleasure rippled through her midsection and down her thighs. "A little," he said. "Your pants are wet."

"I know. It feels icky." She cupped both sides of his face and kissed him. This time he kissed her back, softly and luxuriously slow. Kissing him was a tall glass of ice water on a hot day. It was spring rain and expensive chocolate and unexpected music rolled into one. He tugged her hips, drawing her closer, but she resisted. "I don't want to mess up your uniform."

His pupils dilated, drawing her in, coaxing her away from reality and into the realm where only he existed. She knew they had no future. She could not stay. He could not turn his back on his entire life. And yet, the sky was a perfect turquoise bowl above them and the creek sang a seductive song and he smelled so good and, for a while at least, their troubles were far away.

She stepped away. He tried to draw her back, but when she began unbuttoning her shirt, his efforts halted. One eyebrow arched and she adored the way he did that. He watched her fingers with intense fascination. The damp chambray squeaked faintly as she pulled the buttons free.

This was wrong on so many levels, but she refused to heed reason. Refused to care about the afterward, or the before. She watched him watch her and took great pleasure when she slipped the shirt off her shoulders, baring her torso, and his lips parted to release an appreciative sigh.

He raised a hand. Her muscles tensed in anticipation.

Her breasts ached for his touch. He touched the scar that arced over her belly under her ribs.

"How?" he asked.

She didn't want to bother with the old story about her mother losing her temper and swiping Madeline across the belly with a hot iron. "I don't know," she said. "It happened when I was too little to remember."

He touched the locket where it hung squarely between her breasts. Heat tingled just under the skin. "This?"

"Ugly, isn't it?"

"Not really, just odd."

She wasn't going to say her father had made it. Her father didn't belong in this place. She dangled the shirt from a finger. "I need to rinse my shirt." She headed for the stream. Alive with the sensation of her hips rolling, knowing he watched, her skin flushed as much with happiness as with the feel of the sun.

He walked across dried weeds and gravel, crunching them. She grinned. He wasn't so silent of step now. At the creek's edge, she wrestled free the metal button on her jeans and tugged down the zipper. She wanted to do a graceful striptease, but wet denim precluded grace. She counted herself lucky for managing to not fall on her face.

His breathing was rough, a sexy melody. She got the jeans legs turned right side out and draped them over a bush. She pulled off her panties and crouched to rinse them and the shirt in the clean running water.

"Madeline," Carson whispered. "What are you doing to me?"

Making you forget, she thought, *for a few moments anyway.* She took her time laying out the panties and shirt on the bush. She never looked at him, but imagined his hot stare, imagined his arousal and how much he wanted her. She waded into the water. It was shallower here than it was downstream and faster moving. It surprised her the water didn't bubble and steam from the heat flowing off her naked body. She cupped water and slathered it over her right thigh, washing away clinging sand. She rinsed her left leg, then her arms and her neck and ended by lowering herself into a crouch to wash off her backside, allowing her hands to linger, letting him know without saying so that his hands belonged right *there*.

He made a low, groaning noise. She turned around slowly, her body full and light at the same time, everything centered in erotic longing. She waded toward him.

He breathed hard; his eyes shone with hunger. She took his right hand in both of hers and raised it to her lips. She kissed each finger and one by one folded them into his palm until only his index finger was straight. She directed that finger to her breast. Her nipples were hard, erect and his touch was electric. Her eyes rolled back and her breath rattled from her throat.

He murmured something, half curse and half savage moan, and snatched her to him, crushing her naked body, thrilling her with his strength. She wrapped her arms around his neck and he caught her bottom with both hands, lifting her clean off the ground. His utility belt ground against her pubic bone, as arousing as it was painful. He kissed her hard, his mouth hot and wet and hungry. He carried her to an outcrop of sandstone and sat her on a rock. She was so wet and heated her hip joints shuddered. The wind-polished stone was sunbaked and deliciously rough against her backside. She leaned back on her elbows.

"Take off the belt," she said.

He obeyed as if it never occurred to him to refuse. He set the belt on the ground. She lifted her right foot to his chest and tapped him with a toe. His eyes glazed. He licked his lips and his nostrils flared. She ordered him to unbutton his shirt. He did that, too.

"No bullet-proof vest, Mr. Policeman?"

"Only wear it on patrol."

"It wouldn't save you anyway."

She sat up and undid his trousers. He trembled at her touch. She pushed his trousers and boxers to his knees.

"You sit," she said, not with command but open need.

He sat on the very edge of the rock and she straddled his lap. He caught her shoulders, his eyes dark with desire, drinking in her body. She pushed up his T-shirt, revealing his hard, lean belly and muscular chest. She was so ready for him she ached all over, but he made her sit still while he explored her breasts. She was fire, he was fuel and if he didn't touch her right now she was going to die.

Finally he slipped a hand between her legs and cupped her. She tried to tell him that was perfect, wonderful, beautiful, but all she could manage was a husky, "Oh, oh, oh…Carson, oh…" Release came suddenly, blessedly, an explosion of voluptuous waves rocking her head to toe, blinding her to the sun. He lifted her atop his erection, fitting her to his body as if some cosmic force created them specifically for each other. She clutched his arms and rode the wildness within until he caught her to him in a crushing embrace and covered her mouth with his. His muscles tensed. She kissed and kissed him, delighting in the way his entire body shuddered and rocked.

He stilled. She slid kisses over his cheek. Through

heavy eyes, she studied his face, so handsome it hurt to look at him, and felt rather proud of the dazed satisfaction in his eyes.

Reality refused to stay away. One knee burned from scraping against rock. Sharp gravel poked her feet. She ran her hands over his chest, savoring the sensation of hairs tickling her palms. She tugged down his T-shirt. She pulled from his lap and stood. What had been so sexy only moments before was now undignified. She bit back the urge to laugh.

"Madeline," he whispered, melting her with his sleepy grin. "I'm on duty, sweetheart."

"Oh yeah, and you do your duty so well." Her legs were rubbery and she had to concentrate on every step. She retrieved the panties from the bush. The thin nylon was dry. The shirt was not and putting it on raised goose bumps.

"Rosie?"

The mare was gone. Apparently the noon sun and a pair of humans too enamored with each other to pay heed were enough for her to break training. With his trousers up and his shirttails flapping, Carson jogged up the trail, calling for the horse. Madeline slapped dirt off her feet then struggled into the damp jeans. She ran after Carson.

"Ow, ow, ow," she cried each time she stepped on a rock or sharp twig. She caught up to Carson on the far side of a juniper clump.

Away in the distance, her head high to keep from stepping on the trailing reins, Rosie trotted toward home.

"Rotten old fleabag."

"I'm sorry," Madeline said.

"Did you loosen her saddle?"

"No."

"She'll be okay."

"I'll go after her."

He raked back his hair. "Barefoot? Your boots are on the saddle. Come on, I'll give you a ride home in the cruiser." He extended a hand. "She'll beat us there."

He had gorgeous hands, elegant in their muscularity. Tender hands. Clever hands. She was going to miss his hands very much. Shyness overwhelmed her. What had before seemed so perfect and right, now struck her as brazen. She wondered what he was thinking. She didn't want to know. Pretending not to notice his waiting hand, she limped down the trail.

Halfway back to the ruined house, Carson asked, "Want me to carry you?"

"No-ow!" She balanced on one foot and plucked a sticker from her heel.

Carson tucked in his shirt and carried his utility belt slung over one shoulder. His expression was mellow, as if at any moment he might start whistling. She, on the other hand, turned into one big aching, burning, stinging pair of feet. Soft as a city girl, she thought in disgust.

Carson tugged her braid. "Not much to be said for stubborn pride. Wait."

She stepped into a patch of shade. Carson buckled the belt, checked the snap fastener on the gun holster and crooked a finger.

"I'm too big for you to carry me all the way to the road," she said.

"You're half my size. Now come on."

She wanted to refuse, but her feet begged for relief. She wrapped her arms around his neck and he cradled her in his arms. Such closeness was as painful as it was sweet. She had to say goodbye, somehow, before her weakness for him turned her completely stupid.

He kissed her forehead. "If I tell you something, promise not to laugh?"

"Why would I laugh?" A piñon branch slapped her shoulder. She snuggled into his neck.

"'Cause it's not…I don't know, manly."

He could dress out in full drag and still be manly. "What is it?"

"Before you, Jill was the only one."

She lifted her head and tried to see his eyes. He focused on the trail. Sweat trickled from his brow. "Only one what?"

"Woman. Lovemaking."

"You're kidding."

"You promised not to laugh."

"I'm not laughing. I'm amazed." She refused to tally her sexual partners. She couldn't call them lovers or call what they'd done lovemaking. It was expediency, or loneliness, or gratitude, or lust, but never love. Carson was different. She didn't love him, she couldn't love him, but what had just happened was more than sex.

"Jill and I knew each other from childhood. She was always the one for me. In high school and college we broke up a few times, tried dating others, but no other girl was Jill."

He could have chopped off her arms with a machete and it couldn't hurt worse. *No other girl was Jill.* Madeline wasn't Jill. Never would be, never could be. His meaning couldn't be clearer if he put up a neon sign. His heart would forever belong to his late wife.

As CARSON PREDICTED Rosie waited at home. If he'd been thinking, he'd have warned Madeline to tie the horse to a branch. Patience had never been the mare's virtue. He peeked at Madeline and warmed with desire.

She was so beautiful with that perfectly sculpted face and lovely eyes. He wanted to loosen her braid and indulge in all that long, black silky hair. He parked the cruiser in front of the house.

He was on duty and no matter how much he wanted to sweep Madeline upstairs for round two, he could not do it. He had to go back to town, back to the station, back to reality.

"I'll slip on some sandals and take care of Rosie," she said.

"She can get to water. She'll hold. There's a reason I came home."

She gave him a wary look. Even as a cop, always on the lookout for trouble, he didn't expect abuse and heartbreak from every person he met. He wanted her trust.

"It's good news, for once. Sort of. Let's go on inside."

In the kitchen, she stood with her hands on her hips, frowning at the Dumb Stuff box and the other box filled with art supplies and beads. She chewed a corner of her lip.

"It was in the locker. The FBI found money still in the casino wrapper. When you got the money, was it wrapped?"

Her frown deepened. She reached into a box as if fearing a snake and picked up a dancing doll made from wood and wire. Its painted face was faded and chipped. "I am not sure what you mean."

"Was the money your father sent bundled in wrappers?"

She frowned and tapped a finger against her lower lip. "I'm not sure. Why?"

"Those wrappers came from the casinos. Every bank in the country was on the alert for them."

Awareness dawned on her face. "Oh! They could have traced it to the hijacking."

"You couldn't have known. Anyway, the FBI finished gathering evidence from your things." He debated giving her the copy of Frank Shay's birthday letter. It would make her feel bad. But his protection extended to her physical self, not her feelings. He fished the copy from his pocket and handed it over.

"What's this?"

"A letter from the locker. The FBI kept the original."

She crushed the paper into a ball and tossed it into the trash. She smiled, but it was sad and she dropped the doll back into the box. "I've toted that box of junk all over the country for years. I can't stand it, but it's art and sacred." She pulled the locket from her shirt and gazed upon it as if it spoke to her. "Do you know what really upsets me?" She used her fingernail to pry open the locket.

Thin rigid plastic protected two tiny portraits. One depicted Madeline as a young woman in three-quarter view, her face regal. Executed in ink, it was as perfect as a photograph. The other was of a little girl wearing a tiara. The girl's black braids clued him in that this was also Madeline.

"All that talent gone to waste. He could have been a successful artist. He could have done so much good. But instead..." She closed the locket with a snap. "His life was a total waste."

He touched her cheek with a knuckle. "There's you."

He longed to kiss her, ease her sadness and earn her wonderful smile. He'd never make it back to work. "Good news is the FBI has enough evidence to justify paying for a full-scale search of your property. They have manpower, sonar, metal detectors and dogs. If it's there, they'll find it."

"I take it they didn't find anything at my mother's house."

"Nothing. No mention of Deke Fry, either. I suspect Frank Shay warned Fry to stay far away from her."

"Figures."

"I have to go back to work. Do you promise to stay here? Lock the doors? Don't let anybody inside?"

She raked a finger diagonally across her chest. "I promise. After I take care of Rosie, that is."

"Okay." He wanted to kiss her. He shouldn't.

He needed to.

He caught her face in both hands, canted his head and kissed her beautiful mouth. She was so sweet, smelling of creek water and salt and sex. He wanted to drown in her mouth, lose himself in her body. He made himself stop. Her eyes sparkled. She touched the tip of her tongue to her upper lip and sighed.

"I have to go."

"If you see smoke from the chimney, don't panic. It's just me burning the past."

CARSON WATCHED a black Lincoln Navigator cruise down Main Street. Dark windows concealed the driver, but Carson knew who owned the overpriced, oversize luxury SUV. Maurice Harrigan had a weakness for status symbols. He was proud of his ambition, his business sense and his wealth.

Carson waited for Maurice to slow, roll down the window, call hello or pull over. The Navigator's speed didn't change as it sailed past the courthouse. His friendship with Maurice had ended when Jill and Billy died. They managed civility, and Maurice needed to stay abreast of what went on at the police station. Lately Maurice acted as if Carson didn't exist.

"Hey, Chief," Pete Morales called. He walked down the steps and stood beside Carson. He watched the Navigator grow smaller in the distance. "If he knows about Madeline, we'd know it. You put the fear of God into Judy. She won't talk."

"Let's hope so."

"Need some cheering up?"

After Madeline, he felt pretty darned cheerful. "What you got?"

"Sheriff called. Results are in from the lab. They lifted a partial print from a shard of glass. It's not Madeline's. I faxed the Harrigans' fingerprints." He snorted a laugh. "Good thing we've busted those boys before. No way would their daddy or the mayor allow us to take their prints now."

"Even if there's a match, the boys can say it's from earlier. Kids trashed the house."

"Could say it, but the lab found traces of kerosene on the glass."

"Let's hope it's Sug's fingerprint and not Matt's. Sug will crack, but Sheriff Gerald could work Matt over with a rubber hose and he still wouldn't say boo."

"My fingers are crossed," Pete said. He looked around. "Where's old Luke off to?"

"I saw him toting lumber scraps. Must be making new signs." He and Pete went inside to the station.

He'd just sat down behind his desk when he heard Wanda giggle. Only one man he knew could make Wanda sound like a giddy girl. Tony perched on the edge of Wanda's desk and whatever he said turned her face rosy and set her to wriggling like a happy puppy. Tony spotted Carson and waved.

He blew a kiss to Wanda and sauntered into Carson's office.

"Are we still on the hush-hush about you know?"

Tony didn't have a subtle bone in his body, so why did he bother? "Yes."

Tony closed the door then draped himself over a chair. "I had lunch with Nick. That is one interesting guy. I thought I'd been around. He makes me look like a homebody." He picked up Carson's brass nameplate and tossed it from hand to hand. "I always thought it would be fun to write a book. Never had time before, but this story is so good, I might give it a shot. How would you like a famous author for a neighbor?"

Carson laughed.

"I'm serious. This is a great story. Big money, violence, mystery, and a beautiful woman right in the middle of it all. We're talking bestseller."

"Go for it, man."

Tony replaced the nameplate and plucked a pen from the cup holder. "Got a piece of paper?"

"You're going to start now?"

"That's me. I want it, I go for it." He grabbed a notepad, turned to a fresh sheet and asked, "So this guy that started the whole thing. The insurance man. What made him come to you?"

"Tony, my friend, I will not discuss an active case. I can't."

"You told Nick."

"He's not exactly a civilian. He's a card-carrying journalist with an editor breathing down his neck."

Tony tapped the pen against his chin. "I'm a nobody."

"As far as the investigation is concerned, afraid so."

A knock on the door and Carson called for entry. Officer Terry Robwell, twenty-two years old and a rookie, popped his head inside. "He's not in town, Chief. Nobody matching Mr. Bannerman's description is registered or did register at any area motels."

Carson looked askance at Tony, who grinned in triumph while he wrote furiously on the notepad. "Spread it out, Robwell. Keep Wanda posted about your twenty and she'll give the heads-up to other agencies. Did you check the rental car companies like I told you?"

The young man nodded eagerly. "Yes, sir. I even put in calls to some of the smaller companies down in Phoenix. Nothing."

Carson stroked his jaw. He had washed his hands, but he still smelled Madeline. He dropped his hand before he embarrassed himself. "I know it had Arizona plates, but I didn't note the number. Okay, pass what we have to the FBI and maybe they can come up with something. Light blue Crown Victoria. Ninety-nine or two thousand. Speak to Agent Lipton."

"Yes, sir." Robwell backed out and pulled the door closed.

Carson held out a hand. "You are not taking notes about our investigation."

Tony displayed a crude sketch of a cop with an obscene "nightstick." Carson snorted and choked. He called Tony a rude name and told him to get out of his office.

Chortling wickedly, Tony sauntered out. "Have fun saving the world from evil." He blew a kiss to Wanda, leaving a trail of giggles in his wake.

Carson gazed upon the pile of paperwork on his desk. He wanted to go home, wanted to see Madeline. Ruff didn't pay him to chase women. He tore Tony's sketch from the pad and threw it away. Tony was a jerk, but he was a funny jerk.

An hour later, Pete rushed into the office. "Bingo! We got a match."

"Matt or Sug?"

"Sug."

Carson smacked the desk with his fist. *Yes!* They needed more than a partial fingerprint to convict the little thug, but it was enough for an arrest. Without Matt around to put a curb on Sug's mouth, he'd start singing even before he reached the sheriff's interrogation room.

"Deputies are on the way to arrest him now. Sheriff wants to know if you want to be there when they question Sug."

He did, but he wanted to go home to Madeline more. "I trust them to do it right."

Pete gave him a funny look, then shrugged and turned away.

Carson wondered if sex showed on his face.

When five-thirty finally rolled around, he had to refrain from running out the door like a boy released from school. His good mood died when Maurice caught him in the parking lot.

"You've got some nerve, Cody," Maurice growled.

"If you mean Sug, you're talking to the wrong man. Sheriff Gerald is handling the case."

"I know who's handling the damned case! What I want to know is why you didn't tell me they were arresting him?"

"So you and your brother can interfere?" He shook his head. "This isn't a prank. They almost killed a woman."

"The boys were with me! All night. They didn't have a thing to do with that fire."

"Evidence says otherwise."

"What evidence?"

"Take it up with Gerald."

Maurice shook a bony finger. Even his hands had lost their robustness and grown old before their time. "I'll have your job."

Go for it, Carson thought and opened the car door. He pulled off his hat and slid behind the wheel.

Maurice caught the door before Carson could close it. "Damn you! I already lost my son because of your wife and now I have to lose my nephew on account of you?"

Rage blasted from the deepest part of him and threatened to take over his mind. He clenched the steering wheel so tightly his hands ached. He sucked air, desperately trying to cool the fire. Only when certain he would not punch Maurice in the face, he got back out of the car.

"Jill loved Billy like he was her own," he said with only a slight quiver in his voice.

"If he hadn't been working for her, he'd be alive today."

"If you'd locked him in a padded room, he'd be alive. What happened, happened. Nothing is going to change it. Not hatred, not revenge, not anything. Blame Jill all you want, but nothing will change."

"It was those goats and llamas that did it. Boy didn't care a lick for cattle, but he sure liked those—"

"Get over it! Llamas and goats and Jill didn't kill your son. Frank Shay did and he's dead. Get over it. Do it for Mary and the girls. They're still alive and they need you."

Shaking his head, his eyes glazed, Maurice backed away. "You tell the sheriff to turn my nephew loose, or else."

Chapter Thirteen

Madeline rubbed her hand slowly over Carson's bare chest. Pale morning light outlined the curtains. Waking up in Carson's bed, in his arms, was so comfortable it seemed she'd been doing it all her life. She pressed her nose against the juncture of his neck and shoulder and savored his scent, branding it into her brain.

"Do I stink?" His voice was husky with sleep.

"Yeah, and I love it." She lifted her head to see his face. "Do you have to go to work today? Call in sick."

"Don't tempt me, woman."

The telephone rang, making her jump. She sat up to stretch. He picked up the handset, but held it in midair, arrested by the sight of her bare breasts. She poked his ribs and he put the phone to his ear.

"Cody." As he listened, a slow smile captured his mouth. It turned crooked and satisfied. Finally he said, "Don't apologize. That's worth waking up to. Good job, Gerald, you're the man." He hung up and laced his fingers behind his head. "They arrested Matt."

When he had told her last night about Sug Harrigan's arrest, tension she hadn't even been aware of released from her back and neck. Now, with both Harrigans in custody she didn't need to worry about a Molotov cocktail crashing through a window.

A little stunned, she left the bed and went down the hall to the bathroom. When she returned, the light in the room had turned pearly gray. Stark naked, she stretched for the ceiling and rolled her head side to side, enjoying the way he followed her every move. "Mmm, I think I'll stay naked all day long."

"You really don't want me to go to work, do you?"

"You're the one who thinks being chief of police is more important than fooling around with me."

He covered his eyes with an arm. "You're evil."

She hopped onto the bed and stripped back the sheets. He was ready and willing and she was more than happy to oblige. She loved the texture of his skin and the thickness of his hair through her fingers and the way he smelled and his fascination with her breasts and the hungry way he kissed her. She loved everything about him.

If she didn't get out of here, she was going to fall in love with *him*.

That thought crept in while she lay in the afterglow, her skin cooling, while listening to Carson shower. Now that the Harrigan boys were in custody, the present danger was to Carson's job and reputation.

She clutched a pillow to her belly. Carson sang in the shower. He had a powerful baritone. She'd never been in love, never even pretended or fooled herself into thinking she was in love. She remained in control, always.

She had no idea how to explain the way she felt about Carson.

He melted her with a look. Thrilled her with a soft

word. Around him, even her beloved beads took a distant second.

She could not, *would* not allow him to suffer on her account.

The shower shut off with a clunk in the pipes. A few minutes later he walked into the bedroom, naked and pointedly not looking to see the effect he had on her.

I am such a slut, she thought and stifled a giggle.

He was gorgeous, with long legs and a narrow waist and well-defined muscles in his back and shoulders. Her hips loosened just looking at him. It wasn't until he had on his trousers and was buttoning his uniform shirt that she trusted herself to speak.

"I guess I don't need protective custody anymore?"

"You're not totally in the clear. Boxer Harrigan, the boys' daddy, is a lawyer. Between him and Maurice, they'll figure out a way to get Sug's confession thrown out. Keep your fingers crossed that the sheriff finds boot-print or tire-print matches."

"I imagine Mr. Harrigan is really mad at you."

"He knew when he hired me I don't play favorites with the law. I don't care if you're the queen of England. Break the law in my town and I'm making an arrest. End of story."

God he was sexy when he talked tough.

"Don't bother getting up. I'm meeting Gerald for breakfast." He caught her chin in his big hand and tipped her face for a brief kiss. "See you later." He walked out of the room. He walked right back in and said, "You're a hard woman to say goodbye to." He lifted her off the bed for a deep, satisfying, bone-melting kiss. He patted her bare bottom and walked out.

HUMMING, Carson checked costs on requisition forms against budget figures. His ability to juggle the department's tight budget was almost as important as his policing skills. Wanda informed him the fire department had responded to a brushfire call.

"Dispatch two cars for traffic control and keep me posted," he said.

Wanda took a step, then stopped and turned to peer at him, narrow-eyed behind the rhinestones. "Are you okay, Chief?"

Well, the Harrigan boys were sitting in a cell, contemplating their sins while their daddy tried to convince the magistrate to release them on bail. The FBI had turned out in force on the Shay ranch. If the missing money was there, the feds would find it. A federal presence was keeping treasure hunters away. Stories about the hijacking had retreated to the back pages.

Madeline was incredibly sexy and warm and alluring and mind-boggling. Making love to her was like visiting heaven.

"Couldn't be better. Why?"

"No reason, I suppose." Clucking her tongue, she returned to her desk and radio.

A ruckus brought Carson out of his chair. A pair of officers restrained old Luke. His army-green overcoat twisted up over his shoulders as he squirmed and twisted. His face was bright red and sweaty. His mouth was wide-open and he sounded like a steam engine. "Chief Cody! Chief!" he cried and gasped.

Carson saw in a glance that Luke was excited but not drunk.

Carson caught the shoulder of one of the officers. "Let him go, Terry." He couldn't smell alcohol and Luke's eyes were clear. "Turn him loose," he ordered.

Cautiously, hands on their pistol butts, the officers backed away.

Luke shook himself like a hound and tugged his coat straight. He breathed hard and his mouth opened and closed, fishlike. Carson curbed his impatience and waited for the man to catch his breath. He asked Wanda for a cup of water. Openly disdainful, the woman did as he asked. Luke gulped it, dribbling into his beard, and wiped his mouth with the back of his hand.

"What's the matter, Luke?"

Luke drew a deep breath. "The mayor's gone crazy. I heard him over at the Big Rim telling everybody he's gonna catch him an Indian girl and hustle her back to the reservation. That's a quote, Chief. Swear to God!"

It took all his willpower to not knock the old vet aside and rush out the door. "You're sure he said Indian girl?"

"My eyes ain't so good, but my ears work fine. Says she killed his boy and he's running her out of town." Luke blinked, looking scared. "I run all the way. Came fast as I can. He's saying she's out to your place, Chief, and he's looking for men to go with him."

MADELINE TIED OFF the knot and wove loose thread back through the beads. She clipped the thread and used a lighter to melt off the tiny bit remaining. The phoenix vessel was done. She set it on the window ledge to catch the sunlight. It shimmered, seeming to burn, as if the beaded bird actually rose from flames.

She practically floated upstairs. Her next project was a sculptural piece, inspired by a lava flow into the sea. She couldn't wait to get started.

She heard an engine and her body responded with a wave of desire, leaving her legs wobbly. Carson was supposed to be working, she should be working, oh, but she wanted him. She toyed with a button, wondering what he'd do if she met him at the door naked.

She looked out the window. A black SUV materialized from the cloud of dust. Her heart skipped. No amount of wishful thinking convinced her the huge vehicle belonged to the Ruff PD.

Maybe it was Tony. He boasted about owning a flotilla of expensive cars. If he showed up in disregard of Carson's request to stay away, she would tell Carson. Tony required a good slap every once in a while to keep him in line.

The SUV reached the house. She didn't know the make or model, but recognized it as expensive. The man who emerged into the sunlight was gaunt and had thinning, reddish gray hair. She dropped the curtain.

She remembered locking the front door. The back door was open to let in fresh air. Halfway down the stairs, knocking made her jump. The man pounded the door. She held her breath, willed herself invisible and waited for him to go away.

"Madeline Shay! Open the door! I know you're in there! Open the door!"

A solid thud made her squeak. Another thud and cracking wood. He had kicked in the door.

There was a telephone in Carson's bedroom.

Wood shattered and the door crashed against the wall. Glass shattered. Madeline had hesitated too long. The man was at the base of the stairs and aimed a gun straight at her heart.

"Halt!" the man roared.

Behind him, another man yelled, "Hey! What are you doing?"

Tony! Madeline screamed, "He has a gun!"

The man spun about and dropped into a shooter's crouch. He fired. Madeline shrieked, shocking herself into moving. She sprang up the stairs and raced down the hall to Carson's bedroom. She slammed the door and pushed in the lock. It would never hold. She ran to the phone.

Her mind refused to provide Carson's cell number. She couldn't remember the number to the police station. Holding the phone in both shaking hands, she punched in 911.

Boots pounded in the hallway. The man yelled her name, demanding she show herself. Doors banged.

"Nine-one-one," an operator said. "Please state your emergency."

"A man is in the house! He shot Tony. He's trying to—"

An explosion of wood and the door crashed against the wall. Madeline dropped the phone and pressed herself into the corner.

The 911 operator's voice drifted. "Ma'am? Ma'am, are you there?"

Madeline stared at the man and saw death. His sunken eyes burned with hatred. He wore a dress shirt, open at the throat, but it was too big for him and the shoulder seams sagged. His belt was cinched tightly because his trousers were too big, too. He looked as if he had recently recovered from a long and difficult illness.

He looked out of his mind.

"Come here," he said.

She pressed more tightly into the corner.

"I am not going to hurt you."

"Liar," she breathed. She grew aware of a high-pitched noise growing closer, louder, more familiar. Sirens. Help was on the way.

"You killed my boy."

Realization nearly took her to her knees. Maurice Harrigan. She shook her head again and tried to speak, but her throat and tongue were frozen.

Pounding footsteps rocked the house. Carson yelled, "Maurice!"

Sirens wailed and whooped. Cars surrounded the house. Red-and-blue lights flashed through the windows. Men yelled.

Carson exclaimed, "Oh, God! Get the paramedics! Now!"

She blinked back tears. "You shot Tony, Mr. Harrigan."

"He was interfering." His words were all the more chilling for their calmness.

She had suffered physical abuse from her mother and her mother's boyfriends, and survived. She didn't fear pain. Wounds healed. She didn't fear death. The dead didn't feel anything at all. She feared for Carson. If Maurice killed her, Carson would kill him. How could he survive killing his friend?

Carson called for Maurice and for Madeline. The floor vibrated beneath her bare feet. A lot of people were in the house and outside. The sirens screamed on and on.

She caught a movement behind Maurice. She closed her eyes to keep from warning him.

"Look at me, you bitch," Maurice ordered.

"Maurice," Carson said softly.

Maurice whirled and fired. Madeline clapped her hands over her ears and tried to scream, but it lodged in her throat.

"Damn it, Maurice," Carson called from the hall. "Put down the gun."

"This is none of your concern," Maurice said. "This woman is the reason my boy is dead. That evil bastard killed my Billy because of her! He did everything for his little Indian princess and now you, you son of a bitch, are helping her collect blood money!"

"She's got nothing to do with your boy. Put down the weapon. This is foolishness."

"She might as well have fired the gun that killed Billy."

Madeline shifted her eyes, seeking a weapon, anything to take advantage of Maurice having his back to her. He was so fast. Despite his aged, ill-looking appearance, he reacted like a rattlesnake.

"You have it all wrong, Maurice. Madeline didn't have anything to do with the hijacking. Nothing to do with her father. You aren't this stupid."

"What are you going to do? Shoot me? Here we're best of friends and you'd shoot me on account of this murderous, thieving bitch."

A low male voice spoke to Carson and he replied in kind. Madeline envisioned the hallway crowded with cops helpless to stop Maurice.

"Hold your fire, Maurice," Carson said, and sidled into the doorway. He held his right hand at his side, his weapon pointed at the floor. "When you promoted me to chief of police, the town council was against it. Remember? They said I was too young. But you knew me, you fought for me. Remember why?"

"I wasn't too young to be mayor. Besides, you were my best friend."

"You're not that dumb. Never was. You hired me because I'm a good cop. You know I'm on the straight and narrow. I do my job."

"Arrested my nephews." Maurice's bony shoulders

rose and fell in a heavy sigh. "Can't believe you did it."

"They're guilty as hell and even if they didn't mean to hurt Madeline, they nearly killed her. So don't say you don't believe it. You knew the truth all along and that's why you gave them an alibi. You know if I suspected for a minute that Madeline had anything to do with her father she'd be in jail, not my house."

"You're blind. She's got you whupped."

The sirens quit abruptly and the sudden silence took Madeline's breath away.

"It's not too late to end this, buddy. Don't throw your life away."

"She killed my boy. Billy was only fifteen! He had his whole life ahead of him. He was going to college, be an engineer." A sob wrenched from his guts and his gun hand wavered.

"He's not coming back. I'm sorry, but that's the way it is. Nothing will bring him back. Now come on, use your head. You're the smartest man in Ruff. You say so yourself every chance you get. Show those smarts now. Put the gun down."

"She doesn't belong here."

"Put it down, Maurice."

"I won't hurt her." Maurice gestured with the gun. "Just move on out of my way. I'll give her a ride back to the reservation."

Carson eased another step.

Where before everything had happened so fast, now time slowed and Madeline watched Maurice's shoulders turn. His left arm lifted, elbow bent, balancing the turn. His foot brushed the floor. His right hand rose. His weapon was metallic-blue and the bore looked as big as a coffee can. Carson jumped. Maurice's back arched under Carson's weight and both men hit the bed. The mattress folded in on itself and the bed legs bounced on the wooden floor.

Carson pressed a forearm against the back of Maurice's neck. He pounded at Maurice's gun hand with the butt of his .45 until Maurice's gun fell off the bed. Madeline watched it bounce away and felt overcome with shock and relief.

Maurice grunted and choked. Carson struggled to his feet while holding Maurice down. Police officers swarmed over Maurice like terriers on a rat. Maurice went limp and he was handcuffed and hauled off the bed. Carson shoved his pistol into the holster and scrambled over the bed to Madeline.

He caught her as her legs gave out.

"OH, TONY, what were you doing?" Madeline pushed black hair off his clammy forehead. Strapped to a gurney with an IV in his arm and a blood-soaked bandage on his right shoulder, he managed a smile. It lacked wattage, but it was a smile.

"Running to the rescue," he said.

"Chopper's on the way," a paramedic said, and checked Tony's pulse. "You'll be all right."

Carson stood next to Madeline. He put an arm around her shoulders. "Can you tell me what happened, man?"

"Oh, big guy, it was beautiful in its stupidity." He winced. "I'm out for a run when I see that Navigator racing like there's a fire. Only guy I know with those wheels is the mayor, and I figured it was trouble." He cut his eyes at his wounded shoulder. "I didn't know he had a gun. He kicked in the door, I ran after him and boom, he shot me."

She petted his head and forgave every obnoxious thing he had ever said. "You saved my life."

Tony snorted. "Supercop saved you. Only thing I did was bleed on his floor."

The whup-whup-whup of a helicopter reached the mesa. The paramedics ordered Carson and Madeline out of the way so they could finish readying Tony for transport. When the helicopter landed, it churned up a stinging dust storm. Shielding her eyes with an arm, Madeline watched the paramedics hand Tony over to the chopper's crew. In minutes the unwieldy-looking machine lifted into the air and headed west to Flagstaff. Madeline said a prayer for Tony.

"He'll be all right." Carson squeezed her shoulders. "He's in great shape and I'm sure the bullet missed his lung. He'll be up and making trouble in a day or two."

Madeline noticed a police officer staring at her, a hard stare full of disapproval and disbelief. She noticed a lot of people stared.

Oblivious, or pretending to be, Carson said, "Robwell. Get your evidence kit and make use of all that fancy training Ruff paid for. Collect Maurice's gun and process the bullet he fired inside the house."

A very young officer met the orders with a sullen sneer. "What do you need evidence for? You already arrested the mayor."

Carson went rigid.

Didn't he see it, she wondered. The disrespect? The self-righteousness holding his officers back? The paramedics swept past to reload their equipment. Neither asked if she or Carson needed attention.

Carson had betrayed his town.

"Pete, escort Miss Shay into the house." He practically shoved her at his sergeant.

Pete hustled Madeline inside. She balked, not wanting to leave Carson alone with the mob, but Pete urged her past the broken front door and down the hall into the kitchen.

"Don't you see what's happening out there?" She jerked her arm from Pete's hold and skittered away. "His own men think he's the enemy!"

"Carson can handle them."

Appalled, she stared at his impassive face. Carson's reputation was ruined. His men no longer respected him. He had sided with the daughter of a killer over the man who signed his paycheck. Nobody in Ruff would let him get away with it.

Chapter Fourteen

Carson winced at grinding gears when Madeline worked the unfamiliar gearshift of Tony Rule's Jeep. The Jeep lurched then shuddered to a stop in front of the house. Madeline climbed out. She would not look at him.

"Don't do this," Carson said.

"I promised. I have to." She tried to walk past him but he caught her elbow. She closed her eyes. "It's over. We shouldn't have started in the first place. It was a mistake. I knew you'd get hurt."

He dropped his hold. His belly felt full of lead and his chest ached like a heart attack. "And this doesn't hurt? I thought I meant something to you. I thought you cared."

She opened her mouth, closed it and sighed. "What does it take to get through to you, Carson? Your friend is in jail. Because of me. Nobody in Ruff, except Tony, will even look at you. Because of me. And you heard Pete. Half the town council wants your badge and they've got the other half ninety percent convinced. How much are you willing to lose?"

Everything, he thought, but she wouldn't believe it.

"Tony will pay me to nurse him until he's back on

his feet. Then he'll loan me his Blazer until after the Santa Fe show.''

''You take his help but you won't take mine?''

''Helping me doesn't hurt Tony. His answering machine isn't full of death threats.''

''He's a user. I know what he wants from you.''

Hot color reddened her cheeks and her eyes turned into green ice. ''At least there isn't any question. With Tony I never have to guess his motives.'' She entered the house.

''Don't leave me,'' he said, knowing she couldn't hear and knowing it wouldn't do any good even if she did.

OUT OF COURTESY to his family, Carson confined Maurice in the Ruff holding cell rather than transporting him to the sheriff's department or the state police barracks. His bail hearing was set for tomorrow morning.

''You doing okay?'' he asked.

Maurice was stretched out on the thin mattress, with his feet crossed at the ankles and his hands hooked behind his neck. He stared blankly at the chipped, cracked ceiling. Every time Carson looked in on Maurice, he looked the same. He hadn't said a word since he'd been booked. Mary Harrigan had begged Carson to send her husband to a hospital in Phoenix. The longer Maurice stayed silent, the more Carson thought it might be wise.

''Mary's coming over with supper and clean clothes.''

Not even a blink.

He closed the door, locked it and went down the hallway to the main station. The room quieted when he entered. He felt the surreptitious stares, imagined the unspoken disrespect. Wanda pointedly swiveled her chair so her back was to him.

He picked up a message slip. Paul Imagia wanted to speak to him. Only a short time ago, Wanda would have scoured the building to make sure he took the call. He closed his office door and called Paul.

"Good news, bad news." He was his old frat-boy self.

"Give me the bad news."

"I just heard from Lipton. No DNA match on Shay."

Eyes closed, Carson kicked his feet up on the desk. After throwing every means at their disposal at searching the Shay ranch, the FBI hadn't found so much as a dime. Now with the DNA evidence—or lack thereof— Shay might not have been involved in the hijacking itself, but had only stumbled onto some of the proceeds. All this misery was for nothing.

"But they did find Bannerman," Paul said.

Carson opened his eyes. "And where might that little squirrel be?"

"Thailand. On a month-long photo safari."

"I'm confused."

"So was the FBI until they tracked your boy to the Monument Mountain RV Park where he rented a cabin a few days ago. He had split, but the FBI took finger- prints, ran them through the computer and came up with George Adam Parker of Las Vegas, Nevada. Parker quit his job four years ago and disappeared. Guess who he worked for? Worldwide Parcel."

His feet hit the floor with a thud. "Go on."

"Parker handled the manifest. That's how the hijack- ers knew which shipment to hit. Parker knew when the money would be picked up and which pilot and plane would transport it."

"Was he one of the hijackers?" Carson asked, wondering if the man ultimately responsible for his wife's murder had stood in this office.

"There are witnesses who place him on the ground in Las Vegas during the hijacking."

"Where is he now?"

"Gone. He ditched his rental car. No recent activity on the credit cards. My suspicion is that the heat got too intense and he took off for cooler climes."

"What about the real Bannerman? Is he involved?"

"The FBI isn't saying. I bet his big trip is in trade for information and providing ID and credit cards to Parker."

"What about Jonas Wit? The name from Shay's letter? Has Lipton figured out who he is?"

"No word yet."

A commotion in the station caught Carson's attention. Someone knocked on the office door. "I'll have to get back to you, Paul. Thanks for the info."

"Miss Shay? Is she in a safe place?"

No. Tony Rule was a dog and jealous anxiety made Carson's head spin. Was she safe from Ruff townsfolk, then yes. Nobody, not even Pete, knew she was at Tony's place. He brutally shut down his thoughts, refusing to envision Madeline in Tony's arms.

In Tony's bed.

He missed her so much he hurt. It felt worse than the flu, worse than getting run over by a herd of horses. He was angry, too, at how she had cut and run when the going got tough. She might say it was to protect him, but the truth was, she was scared. She was too chicken to let him care about her, too afraid to let him get close.

He didn't need the hassle, the drama, the heartache. She had too many problems to ever commit, and she dragged around too much baggage for a stable relationship. He didn't need her.

Now if he could just convince his stupid heart.

"She's safe." He hung up and called for entry.

"I found her, Chief," an officer said.

Judy Green's shrill voice raised in outraged protest.

Carson didn't like thinking of himself as a vindictive man. But a crime was a crime and he'd warned Judy.

"Send her on in. It's time she gets a lesson in what accessory to attempted murder means."

MADELINE SET a sandwich and cup of coffee on the table next to Tony. He stretched out on a leather sofa. He'd been very, very lucky. The bullet had struck his shoulder, breaking his clavicle, but it prevented the bullet from spiraling through his body and striking a lung or his heart. He was in pain and he had to keep his right arm bound to his chest, but he'd suffer no lasting damage.

"After I eat," he said, "think you could help me wash up?" He rubbed his bristling jaw. "Shave?"

This was ludicrous. Staying with Tony was a mistake. Leaving Carson had been a mistake. Maurice Harrigan had spooked her badly. Witnessing how easily the town of Ruff had turned their backs on Carson plunged her into despair. What did she do? Run like a coyote with her tail tucked between her legs.

It's what she always did. She ran from her father. She ran from her mother. She ran away every single time she came close to caring. When she couldn't physically escape, she dived into art, hiding inside the intricate mindlessness of beadwork.

"Maddy?" Tony asked. "Is there a problem?"

She forced a smile. "Yeah, I think there is."

"Spill, my sweet." He picked up the coffee cup. "What's bothering your pretty little head?"

Leaving Tony would be a lot easier if he weren't being so kind and generous. "Have you ever been in love?"

"At least once a week since I hit puberty. Why?" His smile turned impish. "Got the bug, huh? Carson's a lucky guy."

"I don't know what to do."

"Funny how sex can wreck the best intentions."

She slid him a look askance. "For the first time in my life I've met a guy who makes me feel good. Comfortable. No games, no lies. He's absolutely perfect."

Tony gazed over the rim of his coffee cup. "It must be my injury. I'm failing to see the problem here."

"He's perfect. I'm not."

"Carson's a good old boy, but he's not quite perfect. Love is blind, Maddy, never forget that."

She wandered to the front door and stared out at the rocks and scrub and faraway mountains. "I mean, he's perfect for me. And I'm all wrong for him. All I do is wreck things."

"I know how you can get over him."

She looked over her shoulder to find him broadcasting his million-dollar smile. He was gorgeous, funny, intelligent, wealthy and the baddest of the bad boys. All he wore was the sling and a pair of running shorts, a combination almost guaranteed to rouse lust and a woman's nurturing instinct. An affair with Tony didn't stand a chance of lasting, but it would be a wild ride. He had tried to save her from Maurice and taken a bullet on her behalf.

And yet…he wasn't Carson Cody.

"I don't want to get over him."

Dust rose over the trees. A few seconds later the sound of an engine drifted to the house, growing louder. Nick Iola's rolling wreck of a Volvo came up the driveway.

Nervousness ruffled through her body and she moved away from the door. "It's Nick. I'll wait in the bedroom."

"You aren't scared of Nick." He laughed.

"No, I just…" Okay, damn it, she was scared. She was scared of everything these days and she was sick of it. "Okay, the kitchen then. I'll make coffee."

Her belongings were stacked, untouched in the kitchen. Tony was a demanding patient and she hadn't been able to get any work done. He was better now. No sign of infection and his wound was healing nicely. He could take care of himself. After her intensive nursing, even Tony would concede they were square.

If Carson turned her away? If he decided she wasn't worth the bother? She certainly wouldn't accept Tony as her consolation prize.

The doorbell rang. Tony yelled for Nick to come on in.

If Carson didn't want her, she'd ask Nick for a ride to Whiteriver in exchange for an exclusive interview. She'd camp out in Nona Redhawk's yard.

No! That was running away again. She'd make Carson listen to her. She'd make him believe.

"Oh, Tony, have I got problems!" Nick said.

Madeline walked into the room.

Nick started and stared at her as if he didn't believe his eyes. "Hi."

"We don't have to bother telling you to keep Maddy's location on the hush-hush," Tony said. "What kind of problems?"

Nick shrugged a bulky leather bag off his shoulder. "My damned laptop crashed. The first real break in the hijacking and bam! Stupid computer is deader than roadkill. I can go to Flagstaff, but you're hooked up and right here. I am at your mercy."

"A break?" Tony sat upright and swung his feet to the floor.

"Straight from my source in the FBI. They got an anonymous tip telling them to check out Jonathon James Garman. Unlike the thousands of other tips they got, this one actually leads somewhere."

"Really?" Tony scratched absently beneath the sling where it rubbed his neck. His brilliant blue eyes glittered with excitement. "Where does it lead?"

"Straight to the top of the food chain. Garman has been giving the FBI the slip for years. Giving them fits, too. He's involved in some major robberies. Jewels, art, rare coins. He knows how to cover his tracks. But they're convinced he slipped up this time. The FBI is sure they can get a DNA match to connect him to the hijacking."

"Do they know where Garman is?"

"That I don't know. But with his rap sheet there has to be some file footage archived somewhere. The tip claims Garman is in the area. I'm hoping for pictures good enough for the locals to recognize. I'd give my right arm to be there when the FBI arrests him."

Filled with rising hope, Madeline stared at the reporter. If he had his facts right, then the end of all this madness was near.

Tony assured Nick he was free to use the computers as much and as long as he liked. He held up his left hand. "Hold on a sec and let me check something first." He headed for his bedroom.

''I hope this is over soon,'' Madeline said. ''Would you like some coffee? I'm about to make a fresh pot.''

''Love some. Are you okay? Carson changes the subject when I ask about you,'' Nick said.

A pang squeezed her heart. ''Is he all right?''

Nick lowered his head and pulled at his jaw. ''Truth? No. He's about to lose his job.''

Grit burned her eyes and her throat tightened. That crying jag at the creek had loosened something inside her. Before then, she had gone so many years without shedding a tear she didn't think she could cry. Lately it seemed that's all she did. ''I'll make the coffee.''

Tony strode into the room. He was smiling. He raised his left arm. He held a pistol. Madeline had opened her mouth to ask him what he was doing when he pulled the trigger. Madeline clapped her hands over her ears. Nick staggered, struck his bag with his heel and fell. He hit the floor hard and cried out.

Stunned, Madeline stared openmouthed at Tony. This had to be one of his stupid jokes. Expecting, hoping, Nick would leap to this feet and· cry, ''Gotcha!'' she shifted her attention to the man on the floor. Nick rocked, his right arm cradled against his belly. Blood seeped between his fingers. Real blood. Real pain.

''I hate this sling,'' Tony said. ''I can't do anything left-handed.''

Nick gasped, ''Tony? Hey, man, why'd you shoot me…ah, jeez.'' His lips pulled in a grimace.

Tony gestured with the pistol. The stench of cordite reached Madeline's nose, startling her from her shock. She dropped to her knees and reached for Nick's wounded arm.

''Get up, Maddy. Step away.''

Tony's conversational tone made her skin crawl. She

sheltered Nick in her arms. He was trembling. "Are you crazy?" she shouted. "What are you doing?"

"Don't get mad at me. Nick's the one trying to wreck everything."

Nick muttered a curse. "It's you." His voice was shaky.

"Who needs crappy mug shots when you can behold the real thing," Tony said.

Madeline hugged Nick more tightly and he squirmed. "You're the man the FBI is looking for? No, it can't be...."

"I really hoped we could do this the easy way, Maddy. We could get to know each other, have some good times. I'd love to see you draped in diamonds, behind the wheel of a hot little sports car."

Madeline shook her head. "You're crazy."

"Better crazy than stupid. Quit playing dumb. You want the key. Well, lo and behold, my little Indian princess, I have the key." He aimed at Nick. "Since wine and roses are out, let's get right down to business. Tell me what to do with the key."

He looked like Tony and sounded like Tony, but she didn't understand a word he said.

Those fine blue eyes were hard, flinty and ruthless. He took a step closer and she wrapped an arm around Nick's shoulders, shielding him as best she could.

"Even left-handed I can put a bullet in his ear."

"I swear to God, Tony, I don't know what you're talking about," Madeline said.

Tony straightened his arm, closed one eye and squinted down the sights at Nick. The reporter quailed.

"I don't know!" Madeline screamed. "Please, please, don't hurt him! I don't know about any keys. You have to believe me. Please."

Tony pointed the pistol at the ceiling. He frowned, worked his mouth and made musing sounds. "Crap, I'm almost believing you."

Tony rolled his eyes. "I'm a tolerant guy, but there are limits. Okay, Maddy, IQ test. For every wrong answer, Nick loses a body part."

She shared a frightened look with Nick and rose. She planted her body squarely between the men. "Leave him alone."

"Ooh, tough girl." He waggled his eyebrows. "I'm tougher."

"If you want something from me, deal with me."

"That's what I'm trying to do," he said with exaggerated patience. "Let's cut the crap. There is only one reason you came to this godforsaken hellhole overrun with idiot goat-ropers and big-hair country gals. You want the key. Okay, you caught me, fair and square. I have the key."

She shook her head.

"Greed is a deadly sin, sweetie. It will get you killed. I know nice ways to get what I want and I know some really nasty ways. Either way, I will get what I want."

She searched his face for humanity or mercy. "You saved my life. How can you do this now?"

"Who do you think told Maurice about you in the first place?" Tony snorted. "I had to get you out of Carson's house. Of course, I didn't count on him shooting me. Just like I didn't count on old Nick coming up here. I swear, this whole county is conspiring to wreck my plans. I used to be a really lucky guy. Then I met your dad and it's been one damned thing after another."

Fear clambered up her chest, threatening panic. She choked it down.

Nick said, "The FBI is on to you, man."

"Yeah, I can see all those black sedans and suits ringing the house." He barked a laugh. "Maddy, I can see you have a soft spot for Nick. So I tell you what. Cooperate and he lives."

"Don't believe him." Nick's voice was strained. "He's going to kill both of us."

"You're not helping the cause, man." He made a "move it" gesture with the pistol. "Get my key ring."

Never taking her eyes off him, she sidled to a small table and picked up a key ring. He had her sort through keys until he said to stop. He ordered Nick on to his feet then marched Nick and Madeline down the hall where she unlocked a large closet containing a solid steel gun safe.

"Inside," Tony said. "Lock him in, Maddy."

Don't worry about me, Nick mouthed to her. *Get out.*

Sick and helpless, she closed and locked the door.

"He's fine. Now you make nice with me."

She considered how far it was to the front door and could she reach it before he shot her.

"Ahem. Want to know what happens if you go scampering off? I'll give my good buddy Carson a call. When he shows up. Boom, right between the eyes."

"I swear, Tony, I don't know anything about a key."

"You are the little Indian princess, right?"

Any answer would get Nick killed. She couldn't think of a lie to save him. She swallowed hard. "It was my father's nickname for me."

Tony scowled and murmured, "Hmm." He herded her into the front room and ordered her to sit. He paced back and forth and scratched his chin with the pistol bore. "Your dad, what a piece of work. I don't usually make mistakes in judging character, but I'm the first to admit I blew it with Frank." He gave her an offended look and half turned, giving her a view of his ribs beneath the sling. A small puckered scar marred otherwise smooth, suntanned skin. "He shot me. He left me to die in Utah."

"You did kill those other men," she pointed out.

"That was the plan. Shooting me was not. But he wasn't that smart. He should have disabled the other truck. Or at least made sure I was dead."

"You killed Jill and Billy."

"No!" Tony looked offended. "That was Frank. The dumbass panicked like a rabbit in a dog kennel. I swear, up until Carson blew him away Frank had the luck of the Irish. I mean, I spent years hunting him down. I had to wait, twiddling my thumbs, until the parole board kicked him loose. When he and Deke hooked up, I thought I had them. Only Frank wasn't there."

Madeline's chest was so tight it hurt to breathe. "You killed Deke Fry."

"Well, yeah. First he wants to play dumb, then he wants to scream like a little girl. If you'd been there, you'd have wanted to shoot him, too. I tucked him under the house, got the place cleaned up and Frank shows up in a rental truck. I'm thinking, great, this will be easy. Frank tells me where my money is and everybody is happy. I was even willing to forgive him for shooting me back in Utah." He shook his head as if amused by the memory. "But good old Frank had to screw that up, too. He came out of the truck armed to the teeth. I figured he was going to do in Deke. He spotted me and started shooting. You wouldn't think the cops around here could respond that fast, but they did." He gave her a rueful grin. "I guess when Frank saw the woman and kid down at the creek he thought they were with me. Bummer for them."

Tony's lack of compassion and remorse terrified her. She had to get away. She had to keep Tony from killing Nick.

"Okay, here's the deal. Deke Fry had the key and Frank had the location. That's how they kept each other honest. Clever, huh? When I got the key from Fry, he told me he was supposed to pick up the little Indian princess. It's the only way he and Frank could retrieve the money. Are you following the logic, Maddy? If you're the little Indian princess, then you know where the money is."

Cringing from the pistol, she shook her head. "He lied to you."

"In the end, nobody lies to me." He touched her chin with the pistol. It felt icy cold. "I knew if I waited around long enough you'd show up looking for the key. So come on, Maddy. You can't get the money without the key and I can't get it without you. We'll be partners. I really enjoy hanging with you. What do you say?"

"Maybe it was something he sent me. My father told me Fry was going to ask me for a favor. But I don't know what he meant and I wasn't there so I never saw Fry."

"Yeah, that's what he said. What did he send?"

She lifted her shoulders. "Things he made for me. I saved it all from the fire." She caught herself before blurting out that the FBI had picked over her belongings. Honest yes, stupid no.

"It's here? Okay, then, lead the way."

THE BOX LABELED Dumb Stuff was at the bottom of the stack in the kitchen. As she moved boxes of beads and tools, she debated throwing one at Tony. He was disabled; he couldn't move that fast.

But if she was wrong, she was dead and Nick was dead and, out of spite, Tony would make sure Carson was dead, too.

Tony peered into a box. "What's the stuff wrapped up in tissue?"

"Finished pieces. Mine, not his."

"Show me."

She unpacked the beaded vessels, baskets and boxes. One by one she lined them up on the table. A shaft of sunlight through the kitchen window sparkled and glowed against the glass beads.

"You do good work," Tony said. "Next."

She opened the flaps on the Dumb Stuff box. Cool and calm, she told herself, wait for an opening.

He picked up the wooden puppet doll and shook it. "Is this hollow?"

"I don't think so."

"Smash it."

She swung it for all she was worth against the table. The doll cracked and one leg fell off. She tried again. The body split in half. It was drilled to accommodate wires, but it wasn't hollow. Tony picked through the box. He had her smash some wooden carvings and take apart a tin puzzle box. None of the items concealed anything. He unrolled a drawing. He shoved the box to make room to spread it out. The box struck the phoenix vessel. Instinctively Madeline grabbed it and cradled it against her breast.

"Sorry," Tony said. "Frank did this?"

She petted the vessel's long slender neck as if it were alive. If she died, this was all that would be left of her. No real family, no children and the only man she had ever loved would never know how she felt. "Yes."

"I see where you get the talent." He pulled another drawing from the box. "Ah, come on, Maddy, stop looking so scared. We'll work something out. I promise."

Chapter Fifteen

"Aren't you in enough trouble, Carson?" Pete held on to the dashboard with one hand.

Carson pushed the cruiser past eighty. "So what's a little more? As long as I have my badge, I'm doing my job."

Pete closed his eyes and grumbled. "Doesn't it occur to you that Maurice is lying? He's protecting Judy. She tipped him off."

Carson stared at the endless highway, resisting temptation to stomp on the accelerator and push the car to top speed. All he really had to go on was a bad, bad feeling that was growing worse by the minute. "The man hasn't said a word since we put the cuffs on him. He won't even talk to his wife. And he pipes up just because Judy says she didn't call him? Why protect her?"

"Why suspect Tony? I thought he was your friend." Pete shook his head. "Man, you don't have many of those left around here."

He checked the rearview mirror for traffic. Seeing none, he tromped the brake. Rubber squealed and the cruiser's rear end fishtailed. Pete was thrown forward then back.

"Hey!"

Carson pointed at the side of the road. "You're right. Get out."

Pete grabbed the seat-belt buckle as if fearing Carson was about to rip it loose. "What are you talking about?"

"If I get canned, the department will need you. I'll radio for a car to pick you up."

"This is about Madeline, isn't it?"

Yes! His heart screamed. "No," he said. "Everything about Tony Rule is too damned convenient. The way he showed up and bought that crappy cabin in the middle of nowhere. The way he's always digging for information. He kept trying to get Madeline alone. Tipping off Maurice was a surefire way to get her out of my house."

"He got shot!"

"So he got more than he bargained for. Except now he has Madeline. Shay told Madeline that Fry was going to ask her a favor. Then Fry is murdered. *Tortured* and murdered. Shay goes crazy. Remember Shay screaming he didn't do it? The more I think about it the more it seems that Shay was scared to death. And it wasn't me that scared him."

"But Tony? Come on."

Carson revved the engine. "I have to go, Pete. Get out."

Pete Morales tucked his chin and clamped his arms over his chest. "You're not going anywhere without me. If you're right, you need backup. If you're wrong, well, I can always flip burgers. Drive."

It seemed to take forever before he reached the turn-off to Tony's cabin. A glance at the clock said he had made it in record time. Halfway up the driveway, Pete voiced a low warning.

Carson braked and craned his neck to see past the brush. He could make out the white chassis of a car in front of the cabin. He inched the cruiser up the dirt driveway until he recognized the car. "That's Nick Iola's Volvo."

"What's he doing here?"

Over the radio, Wanda was calling Carson, needing to know his location. Pete gave him a questioning look and Carson shook his head. The bad feeling turned into a prickling that extended over his scalp, around his neck and down his spine. A lead baseball rested in his belly. He'd been a cop too long to ignore it.

"Tony has to know we're here. I'm going to see if I can talk him into coming outside. You go around the back."

Pete slipped out of the cruiser and disappeared into the brush. Carson parked so that Nick Iola's Volvo was between the cruiser and the house. It didn't strike him as a good sign that Tony didn't appear on the porch to call joking insults. He got out and took a moment to adjust his hat, surreptitiously studying the reporter's car.

Bannerman had fooled him. Why not Nick Iola? What better cover for gathering information than posing as a reporter?

He shouldn't have gone haring off with a head full of suspicions and his hands full of nothing. He should have called the FBI, or the sheriff or even Paul Imagia. The house was very quiet. Too quiet. It was nearly impossible in this country to sneak up on somebody in a car. He resisted looking back at Pete.

"Hey, Tony!" he called.

The front door was open and, through the screen door, the house looked dark and deserted.

He climbed onto the porch, trying to see in the windows without looking as if he looked.

Madeline appeared in the doorway. She held one of her fabulous bead pieces as if it were a baby. He recognized the phoenix vessel. Her face was carved from stone, her eyes dark and unreadable.

"Tony isn't here," she said. Her voice was low and even. "He and Nick went to get steaks and beer."

He wanted so much to take her into his arms, to beg her to reconsider, to work things out. Her coldness froze his tongue and turned his limbs to stone.

"Everything all right?"

"I'm working, Carson. You're interrupting me. We have nothing more to say to each other."

Taken aback, he stiffened. "Can't we talk? Can I come in?"

"No. It's better this way. Come back later when Tony is home."

He read nothing in her face, nothing in her voice. She shut him out.

All he had left was the job. His job said, no matter how he felt or how she felt, he had to share his concerns about Tony. He had opened his mouth to speak when he noticed her hands.

She ripped and tore at the fabric of beads. One finger bled. Threads snapped and tiny beads popped loose, scattering every which way. His mouth dropped open. She revered art, held it sacred. She couldn't even throw away her father's art.

"So everything is cool with Tony, huh? He's feeling better?"

"Yes." She hooked two fingers into the beads and

twisted. He darted his eyes at the open door beside her. She did the same.

"Okay then. What time will he be home?" He eased a hand to the holster and worked the snap free. He folded his fingers around the gun butt.

"I don't know. A few hours. Cabin fever. He hates being cooped up. You—"

Madeline suddenly stumbled to the side and Tony stepped into her place. His right arm was bound to his bare chest with a sling. "Jeez! Take the hint already!" Carson saw the weapon, drew his own and a steel fist slammed into his chest.

MADELINE SCRAMBLED to her feet in time to see Carson stagger and fall off the porch. Her mouth opened in a silent scream. A roar of protest filled her head, clouded her sight, made every nerve jump. As if in slow motion, Tony stepped to the side of the door and peered out, his gun raised, the muscles tensing and relaxing in his hand.

Madeline grasped the phoenix vessel by the neck and swung it with all her strength. It glanced off Tony's skull and he lurched to one knee.

She screamed in rage and grief. She hit him on the shoulder, directly above the broken clavicle and Tony howled. She hit him again and again on the arms and shoulder and head and back. Blood and beads splattered against the door and the floor and the walls. The vessel snapped and the heavy body thudded against the door.

"Halt!"

Teeth bared, armed only with the broken neck of the vessel, she spun to face the new threat. Tears blurred her vision; grief blurred her reason.

"Madeline!"

It took her several seconds to recognize Pete Morales. He had entered the house through the back door. He crouched in the doorway to the kitchen. He held a pistol in both hands, his elbows locked. For a terrifying moment Madeline thought he was going to shoot her. Then she realized he aimed at Tony who lay still behind her.

"He—he—shot—Carson—ohmygod Carson!" She turned too fast and tripped over Tony. Arms windmilling, she struggled for balance. She caught herself on her hands. She glimpsed Tony's hand snake toward his weapon. He looked up from the corner of his eye. He acted far more injured than he actually was.

"He's got a gun!"

A wasp zinged past her ear. Then she heard the gunshot and saw the muzzle flash. With frightening speed, Tony rolled and fired again. Madeline dived to the floor and clamped her arms over her head.

Tony pulled into a crouch. He jerked his right arm free of the sling and held the gun in his right hand. With his left, he grabbed Madeline's braid, looping it around his hand in a bull-rider's rope grip.

"Show yourself or I'll shoot her!"

Madeline squirmed and struggled, but he hauled her by the hair to her feet.

"You'll pay for that," Tony said, each syllable cracking ice. He gave her hair a vicious jerk that made her cry out. "You hurt me, you bitch! Morales! Quit hiding in my kitchen and show yourself. You have to the count of three, then I blow her brains out. One." He shoved the pistol bore against her ear. "Two!" He backed toward the front door, dragging Madeline with him.

A metallic click like a nuclear bomb against her ear. *Crack!*

White lightning exploded in Madeline's head. A great weight toppled her to the floor. Her chin cracked against the wood and stars filled her vision. Stunned, wondering why being dead felt exactly like being alive, she struggled for air.

"Madeline."

Carson! Oh God, she was in heaven and he was here. Hinges squeaked. The floor vibrated beneath her cheek. A man grunted and the weight left her. She grew aware that the back of her head felt as if she'd been hit with a hammer and her chin was bleeding. Hands grasped her arm, helped her upright. She staggered and strong arms caught her.

Her vision cleared and she stared in wonder at Carson's face. "Are we dead?" she whispered. "Oh, Carson, I never got to tell you I love you."

He hugged her to him in a tight embrace and stroked the back of her head and rocked her. "I know, baby. I know."

IN THE RUFF MEDICAL CENTER Madeline sat on the edge of the examination table. She accepted gratefully the ice pack the nurse handed her. When Carson shot Tony, Tony's forehead had slammed against the back of Madeline's skull. She had a mild concussion, a ferocious headache and a goose egg. The doctor put three stitches in her chin and gave her a long list of symptoms to watch out for. Gingerly she pressed ice against her head.

Carson sat on the adjoining exam table. He, too, accepted an ice pack. A bullet-proof vest had prevented the bullet from entering his chest, but a bruise the size of a dinner plate was forming below his right nipple.

"Knock, knock," Pete called.

"Come on in," Carson said. He grunted with the effort.

Madeline couldn't take her eyes off him. If she did, he might disappear. He might actually be dead.

Pete entered and the nurse nodded before she left. "The sheriff is at the scene. I take it you two will live?"

"Looks like it."

Hands on his hips, Pete gazed solemnly at Madeline. "Thanks. I thought he was unconscious until you warned me about the gun. Thank you very much."

"You're welcome." Then she remembered. "Oh, my God! Nick! Tony shot him and locked him in a closet and—"

"We got him. He's okay. He's being airlifted to the trauma center in Phoenix as we speak. It looks like his arm is messed up pretty good and he'll need surgery to put it back together, but he's nowhere close to dying." He turned to Carson. "How are you doing, Chief? Bust some ribs?"

"Doc says no, but I know he's lying. Madeline, honey, are you up to giving Pete a statement? What happened before I got there?"

She told them how Nick had shown up to use the computer to research a guy named Jonathon Garman. Tony shot Nick. Tony insisted Madeline knew how to use a key because she was the little Indian princess. Then Carson showed up and Tony told her to get rid of him or he would kill Carson.

"What key?" Pete asked.

"I don't know. I think he got it from Deke Fry. My father knew better than to get anywhere near my mother, so he sent Deke to Whiteriver to ask me for the little Indian princess." She shook her head. "It doesn't make any sense. Daddy called me his little Indian princess, but I don't know about any key. Tony broke everything apart and he was studying Daddy's drawings. I don't know what would have happened if he didn't find the little—''

''Madeline,'' Carson interrupted.

The telling got her scared all over again and she must sound like a crazy woman. ''What?''

''That thing you wear around your neck. Your father made it.''

She pulled the locket free of her shirt and looked at it. Then it hit her. One of the portraits her father had drawn was of her as a child—a little Indian princess. She pulled the chain over her head and winced when it scraped the goose egg. Her fingers were raw and sliced from tearing at tough thread. She couldn't get the locket open.

Carson fished a pocketknife from his trousers. He made small pained noises, but focused on getting the locket opened. He pried out the protective ovals of plastic over the drawings. Behind the portrait of the child was a pink paper, folded into a tiny square. Madeline slid off the exam table. Pete edged in close to Carson as he carefully smoothed the paper.

It was a receipt from a storage company in Flagstaff for a unit that was paid up for five years. The storage-unit number was blacked out. In faded carbon copy was a handwritten message: *Nobody gets into the unit without presenting this receipt. F.B. Shay III.*

''Fry had the key and Shay had the location,'' Carson said.

''I'll make sure the sheriff collects all the keys he finds at the scene,'' Pete said. ''Should I call the FBI?''

''I think you better.''

After Pete left, Madeline placed a hand on Carson's

chest, wishing she could will the soreness away. "Tony told me what happened." Her jaw tightened with bitterness. "He's a monster. He was boasting about what he did. He killed Deke Fry. Tortured him. He was trying to kill my father. My father killed..." She choked and had to clear her throat. "He killed your wife because he thought she was with Tony."

"I kind of figured that," he said with a sigh. "And now Tony will pay for that, too. He's facing the death penalty. We'll see how much boasting he does when he's in a five-by-seven-foot cell." He eased a strand of hair off her cheek. "What I want to know is, where do we go from here?"

She wanted to tell him she loved him and she'd do anything he asked, even if he asked her to disappear and never set foot in Ruff again. She feared he'd say exactly that. He folded a hand gently around the back of her neck and brought her forehead to forehead with him.

"I know why you left me," he whispered. "You're wrong."

"I don't understand."

"One thing I really love about you is knowing you'd never make me choose between you and this town."

She couldn't breathe.

"It's this town forcing me to choose. They should know better. Nobody forces me into anything I don't want to do. I'm about sick of them trying. I'm blowing this cathouse. Will you join me?"

She snapped up her head. She searched his beloved eyes for the truth. "What are you talking about? You're leaving Ruff?"

"Only reason I came back after college was Jill. Only reason I joined the Ruff police force was Jill. I couldn't leave because of her, even after she was gone.'' He pressed his mouth into a sad smile. ''I loved her with all my heart. When she died, I thought I had died, too, only my body didn't realize it. You make me see that isn't so. It's time to join the living. Time to start over. I'd like to do it with you. If you'll have me.''

Wretched, stupid tears poured from her eyes and there wasn't a thing she could do to stop them. Unable to speak, she nodded.

Pete returned. As soon as he walked in, he made an embarrassed sound and turned around.

Carson said, ''It's okay. Did you talk to Lipton?''

''Sure did. He can't wait to get here. Oh, and good news, they picked up Bannerman, I mean, Parker. He sang like a lovesick coyote. He was the anonymous tipster.''

Madeline looked puzzled and Pete explained, ''Banner—I mean, Parker was a bean counter at Worldwide Parcel when Garman recruited him to find out when they'd be making a money shipment. When the hijacking went bad, Parker wisely disappeared. After Frank Shay was killed and nobody mentioned his connection to the hijacking, Parker cooked up his scheme to impersonate an insurance man. Then he spotted Garman.'' Pete stroked his chin. ''Lucky for him, he recognized Garman before Garman recognized him. I'm not sure if he was trying to save his own hide or if he didn't want Garman to get the money, but he called the FBI.''

''And Tony is really Jonathon Garman,'' Madeline said.

''Yes, ma'am, I do believe so.'' As if Pete wasn't there, Carson kissed her fully on the mouth.

Epilogue

Carson grinned at Pete's roar of laughter. He waited until his friend's hilarity stopped before asking, "Well? What happened?"

"Does that pretty wife of yours know you're calling me on your honeymoon? I swear to God, Carson, you're thickheaded as a bull when it comes to women."

"She's in the shower. Just tell me what's happening with Maurice." He carried the phone to the window where he had a panoramic view of the Pacific Ocean. The water was so blue it made his soul sing. Or maybe it was Madeline.

"Five years probation after he spends six months getting his head shrunk in the hospital."

Filled with relief, Carson closed his eyes. He didn't care that Tony Rule aka Jonathon Garman faced the death penalty but he cared deeply what happened to his old friend.

"Matt and Sug each got fifteen months hard time. D.A. dropped the attempted-murder charge and went for straight arson. Maybe they'll grow up now."

"Maybe."

"I saw the Sold sign at your house." Pete no longer

sounded happy. "You're really not coming back, are you?"

"Nope. As soon as we get back from Hawaii I've got an interview with the D.A. in Santa Fe. Investigator. Sounds like an interesting job. There's a big art community in Santa Fe, too. It'll be good for Madeline."

"I imagine so. Oh, and before I forget. A fella from Mutual Security and Assurance is looking for Madeline. Turns out Parker told the truth about one thing—there really is a finder's fee. You want his number?"

The water stopped running in the bathroom. It had been six months and he and Madeline were getting to the point where they weren't thinking all that much about the hijacking and her father and Jill and Tony Rule. "Nope. If he calls back, tell him we've changed our names and gone into the witness-protection program. Besides, you know I can't accept rewards."

"Uh, Carson? It isn't for you, it's for your wife. Don't you want to know how much it is?"

Stark naked, her honeyed skin glistening, Madeline walked out of the bathroom. She scrubbed at her long wet hair with a towel. Carson's mind blanked as all the blood rushed to another part of his body.

"Who are you talking to?" she asked.

He looked at the phone. "Room service."

"Two point eight million dollars, Carson. Two point—"

Carson nearly dropped the phone. He was in love, not an idiot. Two-point-eight million would buy a lot of beads. "Take care of that and there's a big tip in it for you." He hung up on Pete's laughter. "I ordered whipped cream."

She giggled. "But I just showered."

He opened his arms for his lovely wife. "Reckon you'll just have to shower again."

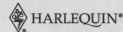

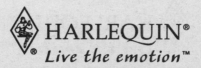

**Return to the sexy Lone Star state
with *Trueblood, Texas*!**

Her Protector
by
LIZ IRELAND

Partially blind singer Jolene Daniels is being stalked,
and Texas Ranger Bobby Garcia is determined to
help the vulnerable beauty—and to recapture
a love they both thought was lost.

Finders Keepers: Bringing families together.

Available wherever books are sold in March 2004.

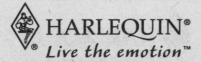

HARLEQUIN®
Live the emotion™

Visit us at www.eHarlequin.com

CPHP

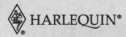

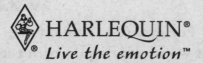

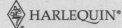

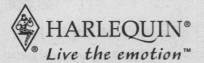

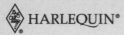

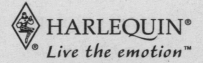